DEAD OF WINTER

THE HISTORY COLLECTION EDITION

DEAD OF WINTER

JAMES GOSS

BOOKS

1 2 3 4 5 6 7 8 9 10

BBC Books, an imprint of Ebury Publishing
20 Vauxhall Bridge Road, London SW1V 2SA

BBC Books is part of the Penguin Random House group of companies whose
addresses can be found at global.penguinrandomhouse.com

 Penguin
Random House
UK

This book is published to accompany the television series entitled *Doctor Who*,
broadcast on BBC One. *Doctor Who* is a BBC Wales production.
Executive producers: Steven Moffat and Brian Minchin

This edition published in 2015 by BBC Books, an imprint of Ebury Publishing.
First published in 2011 by BBC Books.

www.eburypublishing.co.uk

A CIP catalogue record for this book is available from the British Library

ISBN 978 1 849 90907 5

Editorial director: Albert DePetrillo
Series consultant: Justin Richards
Project editor: Steve Tribe
Cover design: Two Associates © Woodlands Books Ltd, 2015
Production: Alex Goddard

Printed and bound in the USA

INTRODUCTION

Dead of Winter was inspired by a famous painting and a documentary about the world's weirdest weather.

Many great artists have featured in *Doctor Who* stories – from Leonardo da Vinci to Vincent van Gogh. M.C. Esher's etchings of impossible buildings led to the collapsing city of Castrovalva, Munch's *The Scream* influenced the Silents, and the painting *Gallifrey Falls* gave the Doctor the key to saving his home planet.

This book is inspired by a slightly more controversial artist's work. If you look at Jack Vettriano's life in one way, he's a former bingo caller and hobbyist painter who was rejected from art school. If you look at his life another way, he's the world's most successful living painter. You'll know his bestselling work. It's one of the most famous images in the world. *The Singing Butler* shows a couple dancing on a beach in the rain. A butler stands to one side. A nurse winds a gramophone. It's an arresting image Vettriano returns to in *Dance Me to the End of Love*, this time showing several couples, each whirling endlessly on a cold, wet beach, vanishing into the mists. In other words, yes, it is pretty much the last few chapters of this book.

You might think *The Singing Butler* terribly naff. You might think it's the best picture ever. But everyone who looks at it surely wonders, 'Who are these people? Why are they dancing on the beach in the cold and the rain? Are they in love? Or is their dance far more tragic?' And those thoughts are what led to the book you're now holding in your hand.

My parents live by the seaside – it's an even more magical place in winter when the tourists have gone home and the town council's turned the sun off. You can stand on the suddenly endless beach and think you're the only thing in the world apart from the sea. And then you start to wonder what the sea is up to.

Which brings us to that cable television programme about the world's weirdest weather. For hundreds of years, mariners have talked about how the sea sometimes glows. A ship in stormy weather will find its path lit up by a helpful brightness from underneath the ocean. In Jules Verne's *20,000 Leagues under the Sea*, a lost ship encounters mysterious 'phosphoric particles' lighting their way to safety. Thanks to science (and dramatically narrated television documentaries) we now know that this strange light is caused by billions of microscopic bioluminescent bacteria known as dinoflagellates, stirred up by storms to emit a light-producing protein called, appropriately enough, Luciferase.

Well, so much for science. I prefer the curious idea that something lives in the sea – an enigmatic glow that follows in the footsteps of the frightened traveller. There is a long tradition of such lights, across land and sea – some good, some sinister, leading voyagers to safety or into damnation. They're referred to as Ghost Light, which would be an excellent title for a *Doctor Who* story.

Anyway, that's the basis for the story. Some magic and a

painting. Now for a little history. Tuberculosis is a terrible wasting disease which proved tough to treat until a few decades ago. The tried and tested cure used to be to send the sufferer to a spot where the air was clean and bracing – up a mountain or down to the seaside. Sometimes it proved terribly effective. Sometimes it just prolonged the victim's miserable fate.

Those touched by tuberculosis led terrible lives. As it destroyed their lungs it caused sufferers to waste away. Fat jovial uncles became tiny, silent men. Famously buxom opera singers became whispering ghosts. The symptoms (paleness, sensitivity to light, and lips stained with blood) led to the infected being associated with vampires. Many tried to hide it, afraid of what would happen if their status was known. Families banished the unfortunates, believing they drained the life force from those around them. The Sultan's harem was patrolled by watchful matrons, vigilantly inspecting pillows for traces of blood, eager to keep the terrible disease out of the royal bloodline.

In real life, setting up a special seaside sanatorium to help those afflicted with TB wasn't widespread until the nineteenth century. But, in this story, Dr Bloom has been able to set up his remarkable clinic a little early and without being noticed. After all, it's the 1780s and the French Revolution is just around the corner. Europe has plenty of other things on its mind. And Dr Bloom may just be about to save the human race.

The era this book is set in gives rise to its slightly unusual narrative format. It's not the first *Doctor Who* book mostly composed of letters and diary entries – that honour goes to Donald Cotton's lovely novelisation of *The Romans*. In the late eighteenth century the epistolary novel was all the rage.

Samuel Richardson's *Clarissa*, Pierre de Laclos's *Dangerous Liaisons* and even Jane Austen's early works all made use of it. It's a great form to use, especially when none of your characters entirely knows the whole picture.

So anyway, here we are. The story of a terrible disease, a curious microbe, a controversial painting, all gathered together in a series of letters set at the seaside. I'm delighted it's been chosen to represent the Eleventh Doctor's printed journeys into history. And I hope you'll enjoy it too.

PS: If you've read the book before and have lost sleep wondering why a certain thing happens at the end which is remarkably like a thing which later happens in Series Six of *Doctor Who*… I'm afraid the answer is that it's a complete coincidence. Writing without script access, I honestly had no idea until I was watching the episode in question. At which point, I dropped my kebab in surprise (yes, I really was eating a kebab) and muttered, 'unexpected item in the bagging area'. Which proves that no character entirely knows the whole picture.

James Goss
September 2014

To my beloved Perdita
Nothing can replace you
— Johann

WHAT AMY FORGOT

The TARDIS was crashing. The big clue was that the floor lurched at a sixty-degree angle. I knew this because the Doctor pointed it out.

'Sixty degrees!' he called, like he was greeting an old friend. 'Amy, this is serious.'

I grinned, and then saw the expression on my husband's face. Rory was clinging to a chair, and making a noise. Making an 'oh my god, you didn't say this was a seafood restaurant' noise. My husband has one of those faces that looks best when it is worried. Since we've been travelling in the TARDIS he's looked worried a lot.

'Relax!' I cried. 'We've done sixty degrees before, haven't we, Doctor?'

'Oh yeah, heaps,' agreed the Doctor as the TARDIS's time engines made a noise like a crashing steam train. 'Well, perhaps not sixty degrees. Not for a while.' A small fire started on the control console. 'Hum,' he sighed sadly. 'The temporal couplings are burning out. Still, what else can you expect? Sixty degrees is serious stuff.'

'Right,' muttered Rory just loudly enough to carry over the sound of an exploding time machine.

The Doctor wrapped his arm desperately around the giant crystal pillar at the heart of the TARDIS. It was glowing an unhealthy colour. If it was a girl on a hen-do, I'd say the TARDIS was about thirty seconds away from crying, 'Hold me hair, Sharon.' Steam was rising around the Doctor's hands. 'Grab on to something!' he yelled.

Rory was about to say, 'But I am grabbing on—' when the entire inside of the TARDIS performed an advanced roller-coaster move. The room spun like a washing machine, in a tumble of brass, books and alien machinery, and then stopped. Wrongly.

'Gorgeous!' breathed the Doctor. 'That is one beautiful ceiling. Funny how you don't appreciate how lovely a ceiling really is until you're dangling twenty feet above it.'

I was holding on for dear life to a piece of TARDIS control thingy. It was seemingly made out of an old banjo. I hoped it wasn't something important. I could already feel it snapping under my weight.

'Why is this happening?' I shouted.

'Yeah!' said Rory. I was suddenly aware how far away from me he was, wedged into the staircase.

The Doctor looked at us both seriously. 'Can't really tell, not at the moment.' He was still upside down like a tweedy praying mantis, clinging to the crystal pillar, which was now rather the wrong shade of red. 'What I can tell you is that we are definitely still crashing, and that the time rotor is getting quite hot.' He looked at me. 'Sorry. I don't suppose you can reach the warp transfer coil, can you, Pond?' He paused and repeated, louder: 'The Warp Transfer Coil.'

'Shout as loud as you like.' I glared at him. 'Still not a clue what you're talking about.'

'Hey-ho,' said the Doctor, somehow managing to shrug.

Something else exploded, and the ship lurched again. You know that terrible feeling on an airplane when you hit turbulence and suddenly remember that you're in a thin metal tube that really has very little business being miles off the ground? That! I could just see across to a large screen which showed us tumbling through the Time Vortex like ball bearings down a drain.

'Something pretty bad's happening nearby in the space-time continuum,' the Doctor shouted over the noise. 'The TARDIS is a terrible rubbernecker – like a little old lady, she can't resist slowing down for a gawp at a car crash in the next lane. Bless.'

'This is not slowing down,' bellowed Rory.

'Good point,' agreed the Doctor, looping a leg around a stray cable. 'Still, on the bright side it explains why whenever we land—'

'We end up in trouble!' I laughed.

Despite everything I was having fun. The thing about the Doctor is that you keep on forgetting there is no safety net. Just one look at him, at the excitement in his eyes, the smile on his face, at the slightly hopeless way he was trying to shin up a melting crystal and I somehow stopped worrying. *Oh Doctor*, I thought, *I'll never forget you*. This turned out to be a bit ironic.

An old-fashioned alarm clock started ringing on the console, a little brass hammer striking a tiny bell over and over.

'What's that?' yelled Rory.

'Proximity sensor!' whooped the Doctor, finally losing his grip on the pillar. 'Which means—'

We crashed.

A Letter from Maria

Dear Mother,

Oh! I am so bored and so cold. Now the summer season is over, there's no one here to play with any more. I am feeling much better now, thank you very much, so please, when will you send for me? I do so long to be back in Paris. I miss Papa, I miss the puppies (this week I think they should be called Antony and Cleopatra – won't that be fun?), and, of course, I miss you the MOST.

It seems ever so long since I last saw you. I bet you must have several wonderful new dresses by now. I fear mine are starting to look awful drab – the laundry here is worse than even Eloise in one of her baddest moods. So please tell me what your new dresses are like, and if we have any new horses, perhaps?

Dr Bloom's establishment is much as it was in summer only darker and much colder. You would not like it now. You would miss the sun and it is always raining. There are draughts in every room and the fires smoke so much they make the patients cough dreadfully.

You would find the people here most dreary and lacking in conversation. The only new arrival is a fat old Englishman who swears loudly at Dr Bloom and complains about EVERYTHING. Dear Prince Boris has taken to his rooms. And the others are all so quiet. I don't want to talk to them much.

What I meant to say, dear Mother, is that I don't LIKE to talk to them. Of course, they are all very ill and should not be disturbed unless they ask to be, I know that, but… they are different now.

If you have a moment I shall tell you how. But if I do, then I should like you to be brave for me. You might find what I say frightening, but I don't wish you to.

Dr Bloom continues with his Fresh Sea Air Cure for the worst patients – you remember how it was in summer? The parade of nurses wheeling everyone down to the beach and leaving them? Well, it's still the same, even in winter. Madame Bloom says that the chill freezes the bad out of the lungs, but it can't be good, surely, to leave them sat there from dawn till dusk, can it? The light is so meagre and the fog is so thick. They look like the Dead. I can't help it – I know you told me not to call them that. The Dead sitting waiting on the beach.

But that is not the frightening thing, Mother. Sometimes I go down to them, to keep them company. But the Dead are not alone. For there is something in the mist and it talks to them.

There! I've said it.

Oh Mother, it scares me dreadfully. Please let me come home. Write soon with news.

Your ever loving

Maria

WHAT AMY REMEMBERED

I woke up. I immediately wished I hadn't. My head spun and it took a while before I could see where I was. It was a very white room, and there was a little girl sat on my bed. She was dressed like she was in *Cranford*, only without the bonnet.

'Ah!' she exclaimed, clapping delightedly. Houston, we have a clapper. Could be exhausting. 'You're awake! I'm so pleased, Mademoiselle.' She sounded French. Interesting.

'Yes,' I croaked. My throat was dry.

She passed me a glass of water.

'Who are you?' she asked, her eyes as wide as curious spoons.

That floored me for a second. I was not entirely sure. I could remember... hmm. Not much, actually. Oh dear.

'I'm Maria,' announced the girl importantly, chewing at her hair, which was really, really long and golden. Like she did adverts. She stared at me. 'I am 11.' She waited for me to say something.

'Right.' I sipped the water and played for time. I was feeling a rising panic. What was my name?

'You can't remember, can you?' Maria smiled slyly. 'They said you might not.' She giggled like it was funny.

'Who said I might not remember?'

'People,' she shrugged. 'I heard people talking in the corridor. You're new here. We don't have many new visitors. So there is bound to be talk. But I'm ever so pleased you're here. I do hope you'll be fun. Do you like to play games?'

I was a bit fazed by that. Frankly, the sense of rising panic wasn't really helping. I tried smiling at her, but it all went a bit wonky.

'Yeah,' I said eventually. 'I do like games. Did they say what happened to me?'

Maria tilted her head to one side. 'Your carriage crashed, apparently. They brought you in this morning.'

That made sense. Kind of. I could remember something vaguely about that – about the world turning over and a big thump but... that wasn't everything. There was something else. Wet sand.

I craned to look out of the window. I could only see grey sky and a few twiggy trees blown about in the wind. But I could hear...

'Are we near the sea?'

Maria nodded, solemnly. 'Oh yes. St Christophe is a resort. It is very fashionable and most expensive. People come here from all over France and Italy.'

I struggled up in bed. 'So this is a hotel?'

Maria giggled, her hand clasped over her mouth, 'Of sorts, yes. A hotel for the dead.'

Well, that floored me. It did not sound good.

'What do you mean?' I narrowed my eyes until it hurt my head, so I stopped.

'The dying come here.' She pulled a face. 'I mean, they hope to get better. But they're dead, really. Some do go home, they're the lucky ones. Mother did. She's back in Paris. Did I tell you we live in a lovely house with ponies?'

Ponies? I shook my head and tried to keep focused. My head was pounding, and I didn't even know my own name and so much enthusiasm and... I was on my own and...

'What year is this?' I asked her. As I said it, I realised it was an odd question, but one I was used to asking. Was this a problem I often had? A memory tugged at my head. A memory of something blue, lying on its side in the sand. Cold water, blue light... wet sand.

'1783.' Maria nodded, clearly proud.

'Oh, very good, Maria, that's absolutely right,' I said, moving with difficulty. I tugged at the quilt, realising for the first time that I was wearing a really rather lovely old lace nightie. I swung my legs onto the floor, realising that the room was very cold. I looked at her. 'Now then, Maria,' I said seriously. 'I am going to try walking. Then I am going to find out where I am.'

'And then will we play a game?' Maria was all excited.

'Quite possibly "Catch me if you can",' I vowed. 'I'll go first.'

I took a step, the world spun and the floor collapsed under me.

At which point, the door burst open and two men piled in.

Someone said, 'Hey! Steady on!'

Someone else cried, 'There she goes!'

Two sets of arms grabbed me and I found myself back on the bed with the ceiling dancing around and around. All that was missing were some dancing stars and the sound of a bird tweeting.

When things settled down a bit I looked at the two men. It was like fireworks went off in my head. One was wearing a suit badly, the other a worried expression and a frock coat. He was holding my hand, checking my pulse.

'Maria!' I shouted, suddenly very pleased with myself and the world in general. 'My name is Amy Pond, and these are my boys!'

Dr Bloom's Journal

Damn, damn, damn, damn, damn!

Kosov found the three strangers lying on the beach this morning, just as the sun was rising. Kosov likes to go for walks. I tell him, I tell him so many times not to leave Prince Boris unattended, but it is like Kosov has a mind of his own. He does so love to go down to the beach, probably to talk to… well, you know what I mean.

According to Kosov, he found the three of them huddled together on the sand, soaked to the skin. I wonder that they did not perish in the night – it would have been a blessing for all of us if they had, no doubt. The girl was quite unconscious, but the two men were just starting to sit up, rubbing their heads and groaning. It was the sheer amount of complaining they were doing that first made Kosov suspect they were English – Ha ha! Dear Kosov is no fool. Lord knows, we've all had to listen to the endless cries and lamentations of that London brute Nevil. It's as if Mr Nevil doesn't realise that he's here for his health not a holiday. The stupid man does not trust me at all.

'Let me cure you, sir,' I begged him when he arrived.

'God will cure me,' he belched, then started complaining about the food.

The stupid man does not understand that there is a reason why the rooms are so well ventilated, why the meals are so simple, and why there is an absolute ban on guests drinking beer, wine, or porter. Honestly, the man is a disgrace, but that's beside the point. Oh, he infuriates me – but I shall cure him. I shall cure everyone! Yes, I shall even cure Mr Nevil.

Where was I? Ah yes, as ever, The Sea…

Kosov could see the morning mist gathering heavy around them and acted quickly before it could settle on them – the men could just about support each other, and he carried the girl all the way back here himself. Imagine it – that lumbering giant lugging her in like a bundle of firewood! I'd barely started my breakfast when he came in with her, those two gibbering fools staggering in behind him.

'What is the meaning of this, Kosov?' I heard myself demand (oh dear, oh dear, when did I get so pompous?), already leaping up and helping him settle the girl down on a couch. I could see that she was breathing, that everything was fine, and that the two men were very concerned about her.

I straightened up, patted down my waistcoat and smiled at them reassuringly. 'Do not concern yourselves unduly, gentlemen,' I began. 'There is no grave cause for worry. Your friend is in little more than a heavy sleep – probably the result of a mild concussion. Have you had an accident? You are fortunate to find yourself in excellent hands. I will happily place her temporarily under my care at this institute.'

'Institute?' One of the men blinked. 'Is this a hospital or a hotel?'

'A little of both.' I laughed. 'My name is Dr Bloom.'

The man shook my hand wildly. 'And I am Doctor…'

He paused, and his face creased. 'Oh dear,' he sighed. 'Well, perhaps just "Doctor" for the moment. I'm sure the rest will come back to me.'

I arched an eyebrow. 'You are also a medical man?'

He nodded. 'Well, I think so… It's all a little hazy…'

I clapped him on the shoulder. 'You've spent a difficult night on the beach. The weather is inclement for it. The icy fingers of winter grip even the Côte d'Azure.'

'Ah,' said this Doctor, and for a moment he looked as though he had no idea where he was. He muttered something to himself. It sounded like 'Warp transfer coil.' These *Ros-Bifs*!

His colleague – about the same height but with more authority – stepped forward. 'Along the shores of France and Italy. Lovely spot,' he pronounced. The English do so pronounce! 'I'm Mr Pond. Well, at least I think I am.' He smiled bashfully. 'Yes. I rather think we've had a bit of an accident with our transport. Quite an accident.' He paused, repeating the last word a couple of times, trying it out for size and then throwing it away as though it didn't quite fit. He shrugged. 'Anyway, we're here, you're Dr Bloom and I'm sure dear Amy – fairly sure she's my wife, by the way – will be more than glad of whatever help you can offer her.'

He stopped, all of a sudden, as if this was more words than he'd ever said before in his life. His friend, Doctor Whatever, coughed. 'Well, there we are then. Perhaps we could borrow some clothes while these things dry?'

I looked at their clothes. They seemed… actually quite remarkable.

He caught my eye, and smiled. 'Travelling gear. You know how it is. Trying to be comfortable rather than presentable.'

The fool stuck his hands in his pockets with a wet squelching sound and tried to look dignified.

I smiled at him weakly. 'Well, of course. Of course, only too delighted to offer you hospitality. I shall find a room for Madame Pond and then my wife will fetch you some fresh clothes.'

Within minutes, my dear Perdita had arrived, the model of soothing efficiency. She conveyed the poor invalid girl to a room, the men were packed off to a warm fire and some baggy spare clothes, and I was left staring out of the window, down the rocks to the beach wondering what it all meant. Had they really come here by accident?

I didn't hear her come in, but dear Perdita was suddenly back at my side. She wrapped her hand around mine and then settled her chin on my shoulder. 'Don't you worry, my dear,' she said, smiling up at me. 'I've taken care of them. It will all be fine.'

'Really?' I squeezed her hand and she squeezed it back. 'I'm just worried, that's all.'

'Of course you are,' her laugh was so tinkling it could make light of the worst disaster. 'Of course you are. But you're a brilliant man. You've done wonderful things. This is… this is simply an inconvenience.'

'How inconvenient.' I rolled the last word, exaggerating my slight Germanic accent until she smiled. Perdita has the most beautiful smile. 'Years of work have gone into this place. Untold effort. We are so nearly at the finishing line. You know what? In all those years of effort, I've never been scared. Three strangers turn up, and suddenly… suddenly I'm worried.'

We both stood at the window, holding hands and looking down at The Sea.

A LETTER FROM MARIA

St Christophe
5th December 1783

Dearest Mother and the Puppies and ALL the Horses,

We have strangers and they are ever so, ever so EXCITING! Today I met Monsieur and Madame Pond. They're staying here – their coach came off the road nearby, and they were brought here last night. Madame Pond is called Amelia, and she is lots of fun. She says she can't wait to play games with me and likes puppies. She has lovely long red hair (longer even than Cecile the kitchen maid's) and her laugh is very LOUD. She is from Scotland and her voice sounds all funny, but her French is really very good, much better than nasty Monsieur Nevil's.

Monsieur Pond is also very lovely, although he seems a little lost. They're both suffering from bumps to the head from the crash of their carriage, at least that's what their personal physician says. He tells me he is called Dr Smith and I like him ever so much, even if he is a bit nervous.

Whereas Monsieur Pond looks worried and severe, Dr Smith is quite smiley. He's ever so clumsy, and I don't think his suit quite fits him, but he's very good fun. He likes talking to girls – quite unlike Dr Bloom. He smells nice, much nicer than Monsieur Nevil – so I suppose not *all* Englishmen are filthy. Dr Smith keeps telling me he isn't a proper doctor, but Madame Pond clearly thinks the world of him. Monsieur Pond doesn't seem quite so convinced – it would not surprise me if he was *un petit peu* jealous?

Dr Smith and Madame Pond were talking about perhaps playing some kind of ball game, but Monsieur Pond didn't want to join in. He said that he wouldn't be any good. I told him he was wrong, but he looked all cross, as though people are always telling him he is wrong.

Then the door opened and Dr Bloom came in. I could tell that Madame Pond – she has told me to call her Amy and so I shall – that Amy had never met him before. She found his presence intimidating – I have got so used to him filling up the room like a big, cross flamingo. But she just looked at him. I'll tell you what happened, as it struck me as interesting, and I remember that you always found Dr Bloom so *amusant*…

'Ah, up and about, my dear?' he said, clapping her on the shoulder. 'Oh it's splendid, splendid. You're looking better already, much better. It's the air here, quite marvellous. It's a miracle, I tell you. Just fill your lungs with it and you'll be right as rain in no time.' He pushed his glasses high up onto his beaky nose so that he could peer down at her. He always does that – I suspect to make himself look serious, but how can he expect to when he has that ridiculous white wig? He patted it down, but it still stuck up around his ears, making him look like a spaniel. Without even looking at me, he laughed. 'I see you've met our youngest guest, dear little Maria. You must not let her tire you, Madame Pond. You really must rest up until you're feeling more like yourself.' He patted her carefully on the wrist and then turned to Dr Smith.

'Well, I must say, it all seems very, very promising with the patient, I'm sure you'll agree, Herr Dr…?'

'It's Smith, actually.' Dr Smith smiled, bowing. 'I've remembered that my name is Smith. Almost definitely. Good old English name, Smith. Hopefully means "noble, valiant warrior" and not "he who hits kittens with a hammer". You'd be surprised the derivations of common surnames in the English countryside…' He stopped, realising we were all staring at him, and coughed. 'Sorry. Amy is better, you say?' He coughed again. 'Well, it is early… early days yet…' and then he trailed off. 'Dr… er? Now I've remembered my name only to forget yours. Whoops.'

'His name is Dr Bloom,' muttered Monsieur Pond. He was standing by the window, frowning down at the beach. He didn't turn around, he just sounded cross. You remember how Papa would sound when the porridge was burnt? Like that, really.

'Dr Bloom, of course!' Dr Smith clapped a hand to his head. 'Sorry. So sorry. I really don't… I think last night has shaken my head up a bit more than I realised.'

Dr Bloom threw a friendly arm around his shoulder and squeezed him reassuringly. He was making them trust him, and no one should, should they, Mother? 'Not at all, dear fellow, not at all. You're all very lucky people. Why, when you were found on the beach, I nearly gave up all hope of you.'

'Is there no sign of our carriage?' Monsieur Pond was barely polite. I know if you'd been there, Mother, you would have given him quite a look. The English are so rude! Poor Dr Bloom took it in his stride, however.

'Alas no, monsieur. It appears the horses cantered clean away with your vehicle. I am sorry. Not a sign of it yet. But once your own personal physician is happy that you've all made a full recovery then I'll be only too delighted to make arrangements for alternative transport.'

'Um,' said Monsieur Pond. He didn't sound the least bit pleased.

Dr Smith spoke hurriedly. 'Perhaps you should sit down… Maybe you're not feeling yourself.'

'No,' muttered Monsieur Pond crossly. 'No, I'm not, Dr Smith.' He made it sound as though it was all Dr Smith's fault, which seemed unfair.

Amy made a face at me. 'They're always like this,' she muttered. 'Catch you later, eh?'

I took my cue and left. As I went out, I heard her say to Dr Bloom, 'If my boys were at all polite, I'm sure they'd say that we're very grateful to you for putting us up here. Perhaps you can tell us more about this place?'

I don't like going to the beach. But I wanted to get away from Dr Bloom. I also wondered if it was the beach where Amy's carriage crashed. Perhaps I'd see a trace of it, or find one of their horses wandering around hungry or something.

The weather wasn't too bad so, remembering what you told me about wrapping up warm, I walked down the path. It was a grey, miserable day. Even from the cliff top, I could see the beach was crowded.

The Dead were there, as always. They never move, any of them. They just sit there on their deckchairs, not even noticing the rain, just staring out to sea until the sun sets and someone brings them in. I know fresh air is supposed to be good for them, but I just can't believe that.

You know the beach scares me. So I didn't stay long, just until… well, until it all happened again. At first it seemed it was going to be all right. Just the Dead sitting there. Then the mist rolled in from the sea. It was like night falling, the light fading as the fog came in thicker and thicker, wrapping itself around the feet of the patients, all sitting there unmoving as the mist started to hide them from view. I didn't like to watch. It made me feel cold and afraid.

Then the Dead started to talk to the mist. I wasn't close enough to hear what they were saying, but I could hear them talking to it. AND THE MIST SANG BACK TO THEM. Then figures started to come out of the sea, striding through the fog to stand with the Dead. I wasn't close enough to see their faces, only their shapes, shrouded in the mist. Over the air drifted a song, just a single, high sad voice, as though the sea was singing to them.

Then each figure lifted a patient out of a chair and started to DANCE with them, moving across the sand in sad time to the song. Oh, Mother, I had never seen this before – the way they moved was both beautiful and terrifying. I felt my stomach fluttering with excitement at the strange pageant. What if they should see me?

'Interesting,' said a voice at my shoulder. Gasping, I turned. Dr Smith was standing there, looking down at the beach, at the dancing figures. His face was grim. 'I really don't think I've seen anything like that before.'

We stood there for a while, watching the Dead dance with the Ghosts. Dr Smith turned to me.

'Do you want to go down there?' he asked.

I shook my head. I did not want to go down to the shore. I realised I was biting my lip and I know how cross that would make you. I shook my head again.

'Are you frightened by them?' he asked, his voice soft.

I nodded.

'I am too,' he said. Then he smiled. 'You're a clever girl, Maria.'

We walked back to the hotel, and sat down for a cup of chocolate in the morning room. In the corner, the Elquitine sisters were already playing music.

'How lovely!' said Dr Smith and bowed to them.

I told him all about the Elquitine sisters – one fat, one thin. You remember how they tried to get you to play as well? Well, today both sisters were well enough to play – the thin one with her cello, the fat one with her violin. They were joined by the glum lady from Salzburg on another violin. The pale man from Nantes tried to join in with the flute, but you could tell he didn't quite have the breath.

'Extraordinary,' sighed Dr Smith, humming along. 'Quite beautiful.'

I agreed. 'It is a good day, monsieur. Some days, not all of them are well enough to play.'

'Oh, of course, a quartet.' Dr Smith nodded gravely. 'It must be taxing.'

'The Elquitine sisters say it does them good… Well, the larger one does. The thin one, she does not speak…'

'Really?'

I shook my head solemnly. 'Why, no. Her sister says her lungs are so bad she keeps her remaining breath for herself.'

'Ah.' Dr Smith looked around us. 'This is a clinic for consumption?'

'Among other things, yes. Dr Bloom is famous for it.'

'A place where the patients dance with creatures from the sea? That's quite odd, isn't it?' He grinned.

I thought then how much you'd like him. 'I know. Dr Bloom is not like ordinary doctors.'

'No indeed.' Dr Smith's smile vanished. 'Something's wrong here.'

When the Elquitine sisters stopped playing, Dr Smith

insisted on talking to them. Olivia, the large one, made sweet conversation while Helena, the thin, silent one sat scribbling away. Dr Smith kept up the conversation with Olivia, but I could see his eyes wandering to what Helena was writing. Her scribbles made no sense to me, but he was clearly fascinated, so much so that Helena noticed, and placed a protective hand over her work, like whenever Claude thinks I am copying his schoolwork (which I NEVER do).

'I am so sorry,' said Dr Smith, looking at Helena with those big eyes of his, 'but those are wonderful equations.'

Helena said nothing, but Olivia spoke, her lips pursed disapprovingly. 'My sister has always preferred numbers to people.'

'Well, I can't say I blame her.' Dr Smith managed a quite dazzling smile. 'Those are very beautiful numbers.'

Helena flushed, hurriedly picked up her papers, and left the room.

He was about to say something more, but we were interrupted by that angry Englishman, Monsieur Nevil. He had barely walked in and was already complaining about his breakfast.

He was yelling at one of the serving girls like an angry toad. 'This egg is insufficiently cooked. I will not have it left runny again.' He pounded a big fist on the table, making his little basket of pastries jump, and then glared at Dr Smith and me.

'What?' he demanded. 'Have you brought us in a stranger, girl?'

I introduced Dr Smith, and Monsieur Nevil simply barked, 'Ah, another quack! Another sawbones! I'm not surprised that old fraud Bloom has got someone else in. About time too. I keep telling him he needs to get a proper doctor. Not that you look any better, sir. I have provided Bloom with a list of physicians I have personally approved and can recommend. He pays it no attention. Says my condition is brought on by bad diet. Bad diet, I ask you! In this place even a cricket couldn't get fat. Where is that girl?' He swung around, his great cheeks rolling slowly after his eyes.

Dr. Smith winked at me. 'Actually, monsieur,' he said smoothly, 'I hear Dr Bloom has a remarkable rate of success. Are you not joining the other patients on the beach?'

'That lot?' spat Monsieur Nevil. 'I've no time for exercise. I have work to do. Important papers and state documents and vital work that is proceeding very well and is not to be interrupted by fripperies.' He waved an arm, dismissing us.

Dr Smith led me as far away from Monsieur Nevil as possible. We watched him yelling at a grapefruit.

Dr Smith smiled. 'Well, I can see why you're lonely here, Maria.'

I told him how much I missed you and the pony and the puppies, and he nodded sadly. 'I miss my home too,' he said. 'Maybe, one day we'll get back there… when Amy is quite…' He closed his eyes. 'Sorry,' he sighed, tapping his head. 'Took quite a knock last night. Not sure I'm in any better a state than she is.'

'Have you known her long, monsieur?' I asked him.

'Since she was a child,' he said, the smile widening on his face before he became serious again. 'Tell me what you think about the beach. It's really very odd, isn't it?'

That's what Dr Smith is like – his whole face is soft and kind, but he says the sharpest things, his eyes darting around like a madman's.

I shrugged. 'It is what you saw, M. le Docteur. I do not understand it. I don't want to speak about it, as no one will believe it. I want to tell Mother. Maybe then she'll bring me home.'

Dr Smith folded his hands. 'I think you should tell her,' his voice was grave. 'This is no place for a child.'

So I am telling you, Mother. There is something NASTY on the beach, and it makes me feel strange. Nice Dr Smith says you should bring me home. Please oh please oh please, can I come home?

Your ever loving

Maria

What Amy Remembered

I woke up to hear Dr Smith and my husband shouting.

'Boys!' I groaned. 'I've still got a pounding headache. You are not helping. Invent paracetamol or shut up.'

'Right,' said Dr Smith and slouched off to the window.

My bloke perched on the edge of the bed. 'This place is a bit wrong,' said the light of my life.

'It's a leper colony,' said Dr Smith.

I sat up in bed right then.

'Well, kind of,' he added. 'Most of the people here have tuberculosis. A nasty disease – completely fatal. Of course, by our time it's still serious, but it's treatable.'

My husband (trained medic, thank you) piped up. 'It's not even called TB yet is it? Just consumption.'

'What?' I nearly laughed. 'The thing poets die of on sofas?'

'Exactly.' Dr Smith was grim. 'A dreadful, slow wasting disease. For centuries, people mistook it for vampirism. You know…' He waved his arms in the air. 'As thin and pale as a model, red eyes, blood around the lips… Not a great fan of sunlight… Plus, if you got it, your family shunned you. At best, they thought it was just a dreadful plague they'd catch from you. If they weren't quite so enlightened, they figured you drank their blood at night.'

'Nice,' I said.

My husband nodded. 'But this is just about the time that doctors were sending people to the seaside for treatment, isn't it?'

'Well…' Dr Smith tipped a hand back and forth – in a gesture that said 'more-or-less'. 'This place is ahead of its time. About a hundred years ahead of its time. You've got to wait for Queen Victoria until someone sets up a proper sanatorium for TB.'

'Wait a second!' I said. 'That means… well, either this place is a bit special…'

I swung my legs down, about to get out of bed, but my husband stopped me.

'Or it's wrong,' he agreed grimly.

'Exactly,' I said, in my excitement shaking him off and wobbling on my own two feet. 'This is just the kind of thing we love. It's what we live for.' I stepped towards Dr Smith on my shaking pins. 'This is what we do. Isn't it?'

Dr Smith turned around and looked at me, his soft face worried. 'Are you sure? It's just… I'm terribly sorry, but I can't remember what it is that we do…'

'Or how we got here,' sighed my bloke.

'Or… much about who we are,' Dr Smith echoed again, slumping down on the edge of the bed. 'Although I'm getting the weirdest feeling that we travel in time.'

This was quite a lot of news to take in.

I put my hands on my hips and leaned back against the wall to steady myself.

'What are you saying?' I asked.

The men in my life looked at each other and then back at me.

Eventually my husband spoke, gently. 'Amy... we're in a spot of bother,' he said.

Dr Bloom's Journal

I knew it! Those strangers *are* trouble.

Perdita told me she met Mr Pond on the beach. He was standing by the patients, watching them sleep.

'Can I aid you, monsieur?' she asked politely.

'No, no.' He was most rude. 'I was waiting for the show.'

'There is no show.' She was rightly crisp. 'These are very ill people receiving treatment.'

'So I've heard,' said the scoundrel. He gestured around him at the beach and The Sea. 'Apparently, extraordinary things happen here.'

Perdita laughed politely. 'I am afraid there are no miracles here, monsieur. We simply let them fill their lungs with clean fresh air. But now the sun is setting and it is nearly time for them to come in.' She busied herself tidying around them, tucking in a blanket here and there, checking the occasional forehead. She is so caring.

Mr Pond continued with his abrupt questioning. 'But that's not all, is it?'

Perdita looked up from smoothing down a rug and met his impudent stare. 'Monsieur?'

'I've heard the sea sings to them.'

Perdita shook her head.

'And I've heard that people come from the sea and dance with them.'

Perdita permitted herself a smile. The scoundrel!

'Am I wrong?'

Perdita gestured at the slumbering invalids. 'As you can see, monsieur, there is no singing, no dancing here… My husband's patients are too ill to move and are not to be disturbed.' She continued, her voice as firm and hard as it could be. 'Perhaps you would care to go in, monsieur? It is not long since your accident. I would hate for you to fall ill.'

'Was that a threat?' the rogue said, as good as accusing her.

She laughed off his rudeness. 'I am afraid I don't understand.'

'I'm sure you don't,' said Mr Pond sourly.

'Please, monsieur, I entreat you to go in, for your health. You have my guarantee that you will miss nothing… There will be no dancing on this beach tonight.'

'Is that so?' Mr Pond became even more outrageous. 'But what if I were to ask you to dance?'

My wife quashed his impudence simply and firmly. 'I do not dance.'

Mr Pond stood there for a moment, looking at the patients, and at The Sea. It was a cold evening and the canvas of the deckchairs started to flutter like the sails of a ship. My wife held her ground, equally firmly, until attendants arrived to fetch the patients in.

At that, Mr Pond turned to go.

My wife's voice halted him. 'You interest us, sir.'

'I'm sure I do,' said Mr Pond as he walked away.

When Perdita relayed this conversation to me, I was chilled to the bone. There is something terrible about these three people. I know it. What are they up to? I should never, never have taken them in! But Kosov assures me that they must be kept close. The Sea is very interested in them.

I must find out more about them, I must. So I have invited Dr Smith to dinner.

A Letter from Mr Nevil

St Christophe

5th December 1783

My Dear Octavius,

Greetings, etc., you old fraud. How dare you send me here to this school for charlatans? Outrageous! As if I don't pay enough for your quackery, you ship me off here at vast expense and inconvenience to be practised on by foreign fools who speak English indifferently and balderdash fluently.

Do you know their idea of treating my poor old lungs? To freeze the devils like a sorbet! Indeed, that's God's honest truth – if I let them have their way, they'd plonk me down on the seashore on a flimsy canvas chair with a rug and a periodical. It is, need I remind you, December. I would be inhaling ice! They call it fresh sea air, I call it more work for the undertaker.

The society here is paltry and threadbare at best. Accounts are given that a Russian prince is also staying here, but he's retreated to his rooms. I must say, I do not blame him.

As if all that wasn't bad enough, I must share common rooms with the insane. St Christophe? St Bethlehem Asylum more like – there is a gibbering lunatic in a most remarkable necktie who can only run around prattling that the mist is talking to him, they let young women run around without check, and the food… oh the food is disgusting.

The goggle-eyed fool with the necktie turned out to not only be a medical man (no surprise, dear Octavius – you are all fools), but also, to my everlasting shame, a fellow Englishman. This Dr Smith had no sooner seen me this morning than he insisted on sitting down at my table and disturbing my cheese-pairing breakfast (some kind of empty pastry – blooming thing was so light a strong breeze would blow it away).

He sat opposite me, grinning like a simpleton, evidently awaiting some kind of pleasantry. He looked as nervous as a courting spinster.

'Well?' I demanded.

'Good morning,' the impudent man said with a nervous lick of his lips. 'Have you, ah, by any chance been down to the beach?'

'That entirely depends on what you mean,' I checked him coldly. 'If you refer to any beach, ever, then I must avow that I have visited several. If you mean the beach outside this very window, then I must sadly answer in the negative.'

'Good,' said the man.

'May I enquire why you ask me?' I kept my voice as frosty as a chapel pew on Whitsun.

'I really don't think it's safe,' ventured Dr Smith.

'Is that your medical opinion?' I asked him. 'For I am very much inclined to agree. I rather think that all this fresh air is tommyrot. There's nothing wrong with my lungs that can't be knocked out with a pint of porter and a good old clay pipe.'

Dr Smith widened his eyes like all medical men whenever anything other than stale bread and gruel is suggested. 'Ah, um, I would rather… What I meant was that I don't think the beach itself is safe…' he said. 'It is not… I think it's very unusual.'

'Explain,' I commanded.

'It's kind of difficult… But there are… people dancing…'

'Dancing?' I rolled my eyes. 'Some dreadful local custom.'

'And there is a fog.' He sounded deadly serious for a moment. 'It talks.' He looked green as he said it, as though aware of the madness of his words even as they fell out of his mouth.

'Talks?'

Dr Smith nodded glumly. 'I know how that sounds.'

'Sirrah, do you not think it may perchance be the dancers who talk?'

'Nope, it's the mist.' His face was a picture of wretchedness. If he was one of my constituents back at home, I would gladly have had him horsewhipped on the spot, but, as he was a fellow guest at this establishment, I afforded him the courtesy of simply asking him to pass me the jam. Reluctantly he did so.

A stony silence ensued as I attacked the pastry, which was so brittle that it splintered everywhere.

'So, er… Listen,' Dr Smith resumed. 'I am certain that something is happening on that beach. Something very wrong. Please, if you have not been down there – stay away.'

I fixed him with a gimlet glare that has had hardened poachers trembling. 'I will take that under advisement. Good day to you, sir.'

He took the hint, stood up, and went off to ruin someone else's day.

A few minutes later, the proprietor's wife hovered over me. She's as plump and jolly as a barmaid, but not bad looking in a severe Fraulein way.

'Did you enjoy your breakfast, Mr Nevil?' she asked, and didn't even wait for my damning reply. 'If you have settled in, may I suggest you begin your fresh air treatment? There is a lovely seat waiting for you on the beach…'

I held up a firm hand. 'Not today, Madam. I do not care for it.'

Fingers as soft as a peach landed on my sleeve. 'Perhaps, Mr Nevil, you would care to try it just for a moment…'

'Madam,' I snapped, 'the only thing I would care for is a proper meal. Can you provide one? If not, I recommend you shepherd the rest of your flock down to your precious beach. I shall remain here and dream of bacon and eggs.'

She eventually scurried away, and I finally had some peace for the rest of the day. I have used it to call for a pen and paper and to write this missive to you. I am called in for dinner now, and I fear it will be as odious a meal as can be imagined.

So far, Octavius, consider yourself warned – this place does not live up to expectations and merely appears a dull fraud. I bid you good evening.

Your faithful servant,

Henry Nevil

Dr Bloom's Journal

Charm! Charm! Charm!

Put on a good face and soothe the opposition! That's always been my motto. So the easiest thing to do was to invite the wretched Dr Smith for dinner.

I met him at the door, all wreathed in smiles. 'Come in, Dr Smith, sit down, sit down!'

'Dr Bloom.'

'Dr Smith.'

We bowed, courteous. I'd arranged my private dining room very nicely. A merry little fire crackled away, and a tree tapping away at the window was the only indication of the storm raging outside. Dr Smith paused, about to take his seat, and then curtsied elaborately to Maria who was scampering around our feet.

'Good evening, Mademoiselle.'

Maria giggled.

Nervous, I patted down my best wig (there is something about the curls on it that never quite sits right, damn it). 'Ah, Maria is… well, she's very much our pet.' I tried laughing, but it didn't sound funny. How to explain the child to him?

Dr Smith raised an eyebrow. 'A pet?' He turned to Maria, dropping his voice. 'You don't look like a pet to me, Maria.'

'I like puppies,' said Maria, proudly. 'I have two in Paris.'

'Her mother has left poor Maria with us,' I explained hurriedly. 'For the winter. For her health.'

Maria nodded solemnly. 'Mother is all better now.'

'I see,' said Dr Smith. He looked at me sharply.

I nodded, swelling with pride. 'Indeed. That surprises you doesn't it, my dear sir, but it is true. A complete recovery. A cure for consumption! But shall we eat? Maria, my dear, if you'd care to…?'

Maria bobbed slightly and went to a sideboard to fetch plates.

Dr Smith turned to me, curious.

'Oh, Maria likes to wait on us,' I said hastily. 'It's like a game for her, and the Dear Lord knows there are few enough games for her here.'

Maria continued laying the table, banging down heavy plates and cutlery with enthusiasm, if not neatness. She trotted backwards and forwards, humming some silly little tune. 'It's like arranging a tea party for my dolls, monsieur,' she explained, staggering under a soup tureen, 'although a little heavier.'

Dr Smith rushed to help her, settling the soup on the table with a loud crash and a spill. Maria stifled a laugh, damn the child. Honestly, she was making such an effort out of the whole thing. But Dr Smith didn't seem to mind – I wonder if he deals a lot with children back in England? Or, having met Mr and Mrs Pond, maybe he just specialises in the simple-minded?

'This is very nicely done, Maria,' whispered Dr Smith, stooping slightly.

Maria stood up on tiptoe and whispered into his ear: 'Don't worry, monsieur, I do not do the cooking as well.'

Dr Smith looked genuinely disappointed. 'Oh that's a shame. What would you cook for us? I've a friend who likes fish custard. Have you ever tried that?'

Maria shook her head solemnly, but pulled a face. Truly, Dr Smith had just confirmed all the terrible things one hears about English food!

'No, no, I guess it's not to everyone's taste,' admitted Dr Smith. He looked like he could prattle on for hours.

Enough of this. Frankly, it had been a long day and I was hungry. I stepped up to the table, rubbing my hands together. 'My, my, what a spread,' I said. 'My dear wife will not be joining us, alas. Mildly indisposed.'

'Perhaps some other time?'

'Oh indeed.' I turned to Maria, dismissing her: 'Well done my dear. Now, if you hurry off to your room, I'll have a nurse come and read to you. Would you like that?'

Maria nodded solemnly, then turned to Dr Smith and shook her head slightly.

Dr Smith winked back at her. Confound him!

After she'd gone, it was just two medical men together, enjoying a pleasant evening's company. How remarkable, I thought. It's been so long since I have sat down with a fellow student of Hippocrates. A chance to really show off my quite remarkable work. I decided to tell him everything. Where could the harm be?

Instead, the foolish man just wanted to talk about that dratted Maria! 'She's a very bright child.' He smiled at me. Waiting.

I just nodded. 'Indeed, she doesn't miss a thing. I fear we are very dull company for her. But, sadly, we must wait... wait for her to be called home.'

'How is she?' asked Dr Smith.

I shrugged. So he was curious, was he? Well, let him remain so! 'She is passing well, sir, passing well. It's always so hard to tell in these infant cases.' I helped myself to the wine jug and turned to business. 'But tell me, Dr Smith, and speak freely – what do you think of my clinic?'

'Ahhhh…' Dr Smith sipped his wine carefully. 'Har. Well…'

I scented disapproval. He was going to be as sceptical as one of those Swiss dullards. 'You do not approve?'

'No, no,' Dr Smith said hurriedly. 'Consumption is a terrible disease. Considering what you are up against, this place is a triumph.' He faltered, as though stuck for something to say, and then beamed. 'And ever so well meaning.'

I paused, a loaded fork halfway to my mouth. The man was a fool. But even a fool must be encouraged. I smiled at him. 'Go on…?'

'Yes,' said Dr Smith, a little lost.

I watched him, as he chewed on his steak (I found mine a little tough, the sauce a touch strong), swallowed and then sighed regretfully. I figured he needed a little prompting. Perhaps the knock on his head was still affecting him. *Tiens, tiens,*' I said, allowing myself the tiniest of belches, which Dr Smith did not even seem to notice. 'It is true, there is little we can do for most of the people here. So little indeed. The diseases of the lungs, the constitution, the kidneys, the dreadful cankerous wasting… there is so little we can offer them… and yet, and yet…' I gestured around me. 'I have decided to try and do something. This humble place has effected some marvellous cures. Some real miracles.' I rubbed my hands together and helped myself to more carrots while I let the words sink in. 'Genuinely remarkable.'

'Indeed,' said Dr Smith, and appeared to be distracted by the willow pattern on his plate.

He coughed, and then he started to talk. The stuff he said! I shall try and write it down… it was like a summary of our time, but seen from afar. He spoke of how the Eighteenth Century was a peculiarly lethal place. Of how if you and your mother both managed to make it through childbirth alive, and you then beat the odds to make it out of childhood, you could drop dead from hundreds of nasty things… all manner of common complaints that would be cured in days to come with a handful of pills. He spoke of how few people in our wretched times died of old age. He said ours was a grimly filthy period, not helped by the fact that people had started drinking water in large amounts without learning how to purify it properly. How much happier, he said, we'd all have been a hundred years before. Or, indeed, a hundred years later. He shook his head all of a sudden, and stared at me.

'I'm so sorry,' he said, and coughed again. 'Miles away. Years away.'

'Not at all, not at all,' I said, waving it away as though it was a nothing. But suddenly… suddenly I had a dreadful cold feeling. I observed him from over the potatoes and thought about his words. The icy worry wouldn't go. I could see again what made Kosov say our strange friends down on the beach were so interested in him.

He had his back to the French windows, of course. I had arranged it most carefully. So he hadn't an inkling of what stood out there. It was listening to his every word. It was watching him.

'Tell me,' he said, coughing again, 'what really goes on down at the beach?'

I stifled a gasp. It was as though he was reading my mind, as though he knew what was outside… But how could he? I searched his face. He just stared at me. Wide-eyed and innocent as a young whelp.

'The beach?' My mouth was dry. I swigged down some wine, and it dribbled everywhere, going down my chin. Stop this now, Bloom, you are letting him see how rattled you are. His gaze carried on boring into me. Unblinking – I suddenly realised it was more like a snake fixing on its prey.

'Yes,' he repeated. 'The beach. It's quite remarkable. All those patients sitting out there.'

'You've seen them…?' I swallowed. The fellow's directness alarmed me. Both he and Mr Pond had returned to the beach – this was worrying. How much did they know?

'Yes,' he nodded and his smile widened. 'I wandered down there today. Really very interesting indeed.'

'A simple fresh air cure.'

'I would hardly call it that.' *How much had he seen?*

A noise. A light tapping. Anyone else would have thought it a branch lightly brushing against the window. But I knew it wasn't. I knew what it was. I looked up through the glass. With a signal I could end this. I could invite the creature inside. It would make short work of Dr Smith.

Should I? Is that really what I had become? I licked my lips and tried to make up my mind.

I was saved by the door opening, and my wife sweeping in. She looked the picture of health, so beautiful, so kind, so caring. I sprang to my feet. 'My dear, are you all right?'

In the candlelight, my wife shone with a fragile beauty, like a paper lantern. Her hair was tied up in tight ringlets which framed her face with wonderful curls. She smiled thinly, and bowed elegantly to Dr Smith.

Dr Smith whistled. 'Someone is batting out of their league,' he murmured.

'What?' I asked.

Dr Smith looked embarrassed. 'Madam, I am delighted you are recovered enough to join us.'

'Thank you.' My dear wife shook Dr Smith's hand, tightly and politely. 'Good evening, monsieur, I am delighted my husband has the company of another of his profession.' She held up a hand, stilling my anxious entreaties for her to retire to bed. 'No, please don't look at me like that – it's just a headache, that's all. I have enough trouble putting up with dear Johann's constant attention when I so much as sneeze!' She smiled at me fondly, bless her. 'Now then, may I bring out some cheese for you both? I may even add to the fire.' She waved away both our offers of help. 'Servants are thin on the ground here, Dr Smith. We scrape along quite well by ourselves in winter. Everyone is very tolerant of our housekeeping…' She paused.

Dr Smith helped her heap some logs around the glowing coals. 'Apart from poor Mr Nevil?' he asked with a laugh.

Perdita straightened, dusting her hands before settling them on her hips. 'Quite! How on earth do you practise medicine in England, if all your patients moan so?'

Dr Smith looked at her, and then his face fell. 'I'm terribly sorry,' he admitted sadly. 'You know what? I just can't remember my medical practice at all.'

She nodded, sympathetically and motioned him to the cheese. Dr Smith plucked some grapes, spitting out seeds into the fire without a care for his company.

He kept trying to return to the subject of the beach, but my dear Perdita waved each enquiry away effortlessly. Her every word was a kind paean to my achievements, to the wonders of the area, to the crystal purity of the air, the wonderful weather, to her genuine pleasure in seeing a hopeless case go home cured for ever.

Eventually, after coffee (not much improved, sadly – really must have another word with Cook), Dr Smith stood and bowed to us both, thanking us for a pleasant evening. Then he turned and stared out of the French windows. There was not a sign that anything had ever been there. He coughed again, bowed, and left.

After Dr Smith had retired for the night, dear Perdita turned to me. 'Well,' she smiled. 'I don't believe he came from The Sea, do you?' And we laughed.

What Dr Smith Thought

I am the Doctor.

I am in a room. The room is very large and very dark. In the middle of the room is a small box that's even blacker. With 'THIS WAY UP', 'HANDLE WITH CARE' and 'DO NOT OPEN TILL CHRISTMAS' chalked on it.

It is not yet time to open the box.

The room has a window. Out of it I can see the beach and everything that is happening on it. I can see Maria. I know that she is important in a way she doesn't understand. I can see that Dr Bloom thinks he is in control of this clinic. But he is not. Is it his wife? Perdita Bloom, who is so very pretty and wears such wonderful dresses. What about the Elquitine sisters – especially the quiet one who draws out complicated mathematical algorithms over and over?

Who owns this place, really? What is actually on the beach? What is wrong with Amy?

The difference between a really good chutney and a really good jam recipe. That's a tricky one. Both involve boiling fruit with sugar. Is it the ingredients or the preparation? You could argue, very carefully, that marmalade is a chutney. But you'd be on thin ice. Or maybe that's sticky ground.

The box in the middle of the room is very black and very small. It should not yet be opened.

Boiling down fine Seville oranges to make marmalade. Oddly, it is about this period that marmalade was invented – legend has it that Marie Antoinette was ill one day and had requested a fine orange cake (she did so like eating cake). Her cook stood stirring the mixture of bubbling oranges and saying, 'Ma'am est malade' over and over… she was so worried she quite ruined the cake, but invented Marmalade. Well, so the story goes.

Something very bad is happening here. It's like this whole clinic is a snow globe that's being shaken and shaken and shaken.

Is this place a hospital? Just because people are getting better does that mean they are being cured? Depends how you look at it. Jam. Chutney. Chutney. Jam.

I know an old man called Michael Finnegan
He grew fat and then grew thin again
He had twelve lives
Then had to begin again
Poor old Michael Finnegan
Begin again.

A Letter from Maria

St Christophe
6th December 1783

Dear Mother,

Good news! Today my new friend Amy was feeling ever so much better, so please don't worry that I am still feeling lonely. I went to see her after breakfast and found her sat up in bed, a cunning look on her face that reminded me of that housemaid who kept helping herself to the teaspoons.

'Morning, kid,' she said. 'I was wondering if you fancied joining me on a secret mission.'

She was up to something, I knew that. But I didn't really mind, as Amy is great fun and wouldn't ever get up to any harm.

'What kind of secret?' I asked, hoping this wouldn't be like when Eloise tried to run away with that coachman.

Her eyes lit up excitedly. 'Well, it's like this,' she said, beckoning me up onto the bed. 'Dr Smith—'

'I like him,' I said.

'So do I,' she agreed. 'Very much. He's handsome, don't you think? Well, he wants to know if there are any... secret patients. You know, VIPs hidden somewhere around the building. Nothing naughty or dangerous. Just people that Dr Bloom might not want us to know about.'

I considered. 'Not really,' I replied. 'I don't think Dr Bloom would care that much what you knew. But Madame Bloom… she'd be ever so cross if she found you where you shouldn't be.' I paused. 'Or perhaps that's just how she is with me.'

'So come on, tell me, Maria,' she said. 'Where aren't you allowed to go?'

I looked down at the floor, considering. I knew I'd tell her. I just didn't want to seem too eager. 'All right,' I said at last. 'There are Prince Boris's rooms.'

Amy laughed delightedly. 'Prince Boris?' She clapped her hands together.

'He's very handsome,' I sighed. 'And Russian.'

Amy ruffled my hair. 'A hot Russian with the cold dead eyes of a killer? Bring it on!' She seemed excited.

I was doubtful. 'I don't think he's killed anyone. I mean, he's probably killed ever so many peasants, but they really don't count in Russia.'

'Um,' said Amy.

'But he's very nice. He has chocolate.'

Amy fell back against the pillow, smiling. 'Sounds like my ideal man.'

Which is how I ended up wheeling Amy to meet Prince Boris. I found a bath chair in one of the corridors and pushed her quite easily. She said it reminded her of going round a superb market with a trolley. What emporiums they must have in England where one is wheeled around in chairs! I would so like to visit an English Shop, Mother. The superb markets of White Rose can't be as good as the delicatessens of Paris, but apparently the Tescaux family stock ever so many things.

The chair squeaked, which made us both giggle, and it honestly wasn't that hard moving Amy around. She kept protesting and apologising that 'her boys' were 'out and about'. She pulled a face. 'Honestly, when you grow up you'll learn you may as well try herding cats as keeping men in one place,' she told me solemnly, which I vowed to remember.

Prince Boris still has that quite nice set of rooms in the west wing of the resort. Normally that dreadful Mr Kosov is around and chases me away, or sometimes plays cards with me, but there was no sign of him today, so I just knocked at the door.

'Come in!' yelled Prince Boris. He was speaking French and he does it ever so well.

Amy was immediately struck by Prince Boris. He's ever so nice, isn't he, Mother? He was sitting up in bed, reading, wrapped up in furs. Looking every inch how a Russian Prince should look – handsome, noble, his nightshirt beautifully made, and his long beard wonderfully trimmed.

'You look like a yeti,' breathed Amy.

Prince Boris laughed. 'And you are?'

'Amelia Pond,' she said. 'Your Grace. Sorry if I don't get up. Maria, curtsy for the nice Prince.'

I curtsied and Amy nodded, pleased. 'She does it very well, doesn't she?'

Prince Boris bowed his head, solemnly. 'I am likewise indisposed, I fear. Forgive me for not rising. I have been stuck in this bed for weeks, I regret.' He sighed, tossing his book to one side. 'You wouldn't think I used to be an athlete, would you?'

'So what you in here for?' asked Amy. Scottish women, were, I thought, a little direct.

'Laziness!' Prince Boris laughed again with his deep and lovely laugh. 'Oh, I'm wasting away along with everyone else!'

There was the tiniest rattle which you could just hear under his voice. 'My family don't care to look at me like this, so they've packed me off here to be out of the way. Which I am doing splendidly. It's quite a relief really. No estates to look after, no serfs to deal with. I'm reading ever so many clever books. But I do miss the dancing and the hunting and…' he paused, gallantly, 'the company of a pretty young lady, Mademoiselle.'

'Madame.' Amy was firm, wheeling herself a little closer to the bed. 'I'm a married woman,' she said softly.

'Aren't they all?' Prince Boris laughed, again with that slight echo in his chest. 'I've no doubt you are, my dear. So what is your story? What are you doing among the dead?'

She tipped her head to one side. 'Our carriage came off the road nearby, and I'm still a bit the worse for wear.' She winced. 'A bump on the head, but I should be up and about in a day or so.'

'Oh.' Prince Boris has very nice manners. 'How sad that I shall not long have the delight of your company. I should have adored taking you horse riding.'

'You can still ride horses?'

Boris nodded. 'Maybe, soon. My manservant Kosov taught me to ride when I was a boy. Been with me ever since. Even followed me to this lacklustre place. He says there's actually some improvement in my condition, can you believe it? Put it down to the fresh sea air! How he can tell, I don't know. Bless the fellow, he watches over me while I sleep. I should be touched by his loyalty. But it is rather like having a faithful hound.'

'One that does the ironing,' muttered Amy.

Prince Boris noticed I was getting a bit bored of all this. 'Ah, and what do you think of our very own pet here, the adorable Maria?'

Amy looked at me, smiling like she'd stolen sweets. 'She's a treasure. If I were her mother, I wouldn't leave her alone.' I am sorry Mother, but that is what she said! I think you are CRUEL for leaving me here!

'Indeed,' agreed Boris (see, even ROYALTY agrees!). 'But she's here for her health, aren't you, my dear?'

'I'm feeling much better, thank you, Your Highness,' I muttered dully.

'Now, now, none of that. Especially not in front of Madame Pond. You'll call me Boris. Now, what can we do to amuse you?' He cracked such a lovely smile.

Which is how we ended up having a chariot race. Amy objected, but Boris had soon settled her on his bed while he and I faced up to each other in wheelchairs.

'I can't believe you're doing this,' protested Amy.

'Nonsense,' laughed Boris. 'A little light exercise will do me the power of good.' He tested his grip on the wheels. 'Capital,' he announced.

'Don't let me win, Boris,' I warned him.

He looked at me solemnly. 'My dear, I am a Romanov. We were brought up never to let anyone else win anything.' He turned back to Amy, bouncing his chair off the ground. 'Come now, will you start the race like Queen Guinevere by dropping a handkerchief? Permit me to fetch you one.'

A minute later one of Prince Boris's embroidered silk handkerchiefs fluttered to the floor and we were off, round the room and down the corridor. To be truthful, it was harder work than I had thought, my hands stiff against the squeaking wheels and the chair itself so heavy.

Prince Boris had a clear lead and was laughing loudly, a laugh that simply spurred me to try harder and faster. The wheels rattled against the hard floor and I spun them faster and faster, catching up to his chair. As I started to overtake, he gave an enormous hearty roar of outrage and grabbed his wheel, twisting it so that his chair brushed against mine. 'I do not play fair!' he hissed, his eyes FLASHING.

I could hear Amy yelling foul, but I pushed on ahead and streaked off around the corner.

I had travelled a hundred yards before I realised that something was wrong.

Oh, Mother! Will they forgive me for KILLING him?

What Amy Remembered

Prince Boris toppled out of the bath chair, taking it with him. The ridiculous, funny bear of a man crashed to the floor with a rattling groan. He was gasping for air like a drowning fish, one leg kicking out over and over again.

I ran to him, as best as I could, and stroked his vast mane of hair. He held his breath suddenly, like he was trying to ward off hiccups, and then whispered urgently: 'Don't let the child see me like this.' Then a fit of coughing racked him. The coughs were like a great engine misfiring, tearing him apart.

I stood up, trying not to panic, looking around for Maria.

Instead, looming over me was a giant, all beetroot face and red hair. He looked furious. 'What have you done?' he roared, his Russian accent thick as stew.

'It was just a game,' I protested, my voice sounding like I was a naughty 6-year-old.

The man scooped up Prince Boris with ease, carrying him off to his room and slamming the door behind him. The wheelchair sat in the corridor, one wheel spinning to a halt. I gingerly set it right, leaning upon it. I could feel my strength go and rested against a wall for support.

With a pathetic squeak-squeak-squeak, Maria's chair

slowly rounded the corner, her eyes wide as plates. 'Where's Prince Boris? What's happened?' she asked.

'He, uh…' I looked at the door and then back at her. She looked at me, clearly worried. 'He's gone for a lie down,' I said.

She looked at me, her lip starting to tremble. 'Am I in any trouble?' she quailed.

I shook my head. 'No, no, no. He's just tired. What about you? Do you fancy an afternoon nap, too?'

Maria stared at me, unblinking. 'You're a terrible liar,' she said.

I was about to reply when the door to Boris's room started to open. 'Run!' I hissed, and she did.

A giant steak of a hand landed on my shoulder. It was that strange giant and he didn't seem any happier.

'I think you should come inside,' he growled.

A Letter from Mr Nevil

St Christophe
6th December 1783

Dear Octavius, you old fraud,

This terrible place continues to grind me down most intolerably. Run by a pinched goose of a fellow and his hell-cat wife, the food is terrible, and the treatment is laughable.

The rest of the patients are as addle-pated as one could hope for – no doubt you are praying that I shall join them in insanity.

Four of the wretches play music all the dashed day – only it's a mere three at the moment as one has become mercifully indisposed. It is wretched German vulgarian stuff, but then the main players are two dried-up old spinsters from the Danube, the Elquitines.

The fat one speaks passable English and seems quite intelligent, but the thin one simply scowls and writes sheet after sheet of numbers – no doubt laundry lists.

Of course, those two new English guests can't leave them alone. It is Mr Pond who insulted the thin one. He picked up one of her sheets of paper, which scandalised her.

'I am sorry,' he said, apologising too late. 'But really, these

51

are extraordinary. This is amazing work.'

His colleague, the one who calls himself a doctor (but clearly isn't) nodded. 'I was wondering when you'd notice.' He smiled a big fat smile – it's the look I've seen on many a poacher returning home with a rucksack full of my rabbits.

'These… these are…'

This Dr Smith nodded again, leaning forward and returning the sheet of paper to a clearly very distressed Elquitine sister. 'Helena,' he said, 'you are amazing. Years ahead of your time… this is extraordinary stuff…'

'It looks like machine code…' muttered Mr Pond, talking gibberish.

'Well, exactly,' agreed Dr Smith. 'It's a logic gate. You sexy thing, Helena. Why, with work like this…'

Olivia, the fat one, cleared her throat and then addressed this impertinence severely. 'If, gentlemen, you are addressing my sister, then I must point out that she does not speak. My sister has always been brilliant with mathematics. But she had to give up her studies when this disease claimed me. Then she fell ill herself, no doubt catching this dreadful disease while nursing me. Now she can only manage to work a few hours a day. I feel I have ruined her life.' She glowered at them dourly – she's quite spirited for a filly. 'So instead we play music. Which has a magic all of its own, I am sure you'll agree.'

She bowed to Dr Smith, collected her sister, and they retired to their room. We stood to bid them farewell. Once they were out of earshot, I gave those two stupid men a piece of my mind. Such rudeness to ladies! What can foreigners think of we English? Sadly, I think I shouted so much that I have done myself a mischief. My breath has been short and ragged ever since, and most certainly I now appear to be very ill.

Some cure this is proving to be! Some cure, indeed!
Your faithful servant,
Henry Nevil

DR BLOOM'S JOURNAL

6th December 1783

Amateurs!

'I'm so sorry to disturb you in your study,' bellowed Mr Pond, sweeping a hand nervously through his hair, 'but I think poor Mr Nevil is having a funny turn.'

I glared at him. This was all I needed.

I made my way to the restaurant, Mr Pond trailing behind me like a nervous insect. Apparently, he'd been sitting with Dr Smith trying to have a quiet tisane when Mr Nevil had thundered up to them, no doubt having one of his outbursts about… well, anything and everything. According to Mr Pond, he'd been pounding the table about some imagined insult or other when he'd turned purple.

I could see Dr Smith tugging at the floundering man's shirt. Nevil's ridiculous wig had come off, and his giant shining bald pate was as purple as his face. There was froth around his mouth, but that didn't stop him from swearing as soon as he saw me.

I tried to ignore the abuse, and checked his pulse and temperature.

Dr Smith muttered something about blood pressure. It

seemed Mr Nevil had nearly bitten off one of Dr Smith's fingers while he'd been stopping him from swallowing his livid tongue. It hadn't been a pretty sight.

'Damn you, sir, damn you!' screamed Nevil hoarsely, frothing at the mouth. 'I came here for a cure and you have nearly finished me off! What's happening to me?'

'Calm down, dear sir.' I tried out my professionally soothing voice. 'Deep breaths; as deep as you can manage. You've not been following the treatment plan.'

'Plan, pah! Sitting on the beach catching my death of cold. We have quite enough bad weather in England not to expose myself to it abroad.'

'I can assure you, the results are remarkable. You need to trust me.'

'Trust a foreign quack with my health? I'd rather trust Tom Long the Butcher's Boy.' Nevil spat with disgust. I cast a professional glance at the spittle to see if there was much blood flecked in it. Little enough, so that was all right, at least.

We laid Nevil out on a bench, and he gradually got his breath back. He used it to call for brandy, but I waved this away. Then I looked at him sternly.

'Mr Nevil, my patience is exhausted. I beseech you one final time to take my treatment and go and sit with my other guests.'

'Of course I shan't!' he protested, settling his wig again on his head and sucking in breath like a broken bellows. 'It's mere choleric, that's all.'

I shook my head. 'It is not bad temper, sir, and you know it. I'm sorry, but the truth must be faced. You are a very ill man.'

'I demand a second opinion!' he roared.

Dr Smith coughed delicately. I tried not to glower at him, but managed quite a nice professional smile, all things considered. 'Dr Smith?' I asked.

'I'm happy to offer a second opinion,' he ventured. I should, perhaps have clouted him over the head for that, but I merely nodded.

'I should be interested to hear it, my dear sir.' I forced a grimace.

Dr Smith paused, waiting until he had all of Nevil's attention. 'I am afraid, Mr Nevil, that I can only agree with Dr Bloom. You are very seriously ill.'

Nevil deflated, sinking back onto the bench. 'I see, I see,' he gasped, his eyes rolling madly.

I nodded gratefully at Dr Smith, and then continued, gently. 'As I was saying, enough is enough. If you won't try the fresh air cure, then I shall simply make alternative arrangements. Please come to my study at eight o'clock tonight. If you do not attend, then I shall reluctantly ask you to leave my establishment. Is that clear?'

I did not wait for a response, I simply turned on my heel and left. These English! They are truly awful!

Perdita was her normal supportive self when I told her what had happened. 'You did exactly the right thing, Johann,' she enthused. 'These rude men respect only rough handling.'

I nodded. 'I know, I know, but it does rather lack our normal subtlety.'

She cupped a hand to my face. 'But he'll be delighted with the results. Mr Nevil is a very important man back in England. He'll spread the word of your marvellous work, and then more important people will come here.' She smiled, tapping me fondly on the nose. 'And you will cure them all, my brilliant husband.'

I took her hand in mine and smiled up at her endlessly lovely eyes.

'Yes,' I agreed. 'I will cure them all.'

It took a lot of arranging, but everything was prepared by eight.

Nevil marched into my study without knocking. He immediately saw the open French windows. 'Dashed freezing in here,' he complained. 'That Smith fellow tried to tag along. He didn't want me to come alone, blast him. Dashed fellow probably just saw a chance to send me a bill! I will not be mollycoddled. Do something about that perishing draught, though, will you?' He jerked a fat thumb at the open door, swinging in the evening breeze.

I demurred. I was keenly anticipating what was about to happen. 'I'm afraid it's necessary.'

'Blazes it is,' he thundered like a cross toad. 'It's like my nanny, she was always making me sleep at night with the window open. Nearly killed me as a child and I've never stood for the cold since. Nor do I fancy wasting my time shivering under a blanket on your blessed beach. Let's go to it – you promised me hope, and all I've had so far is thin soup and cheap cuts of meat.'

I bowed and drew back the curtain further, exposing the open door, the terrace, and the thing beyond it. The thing that had sat there, waiting for him.

Mr Nevil stared in horror as the thing drifted and crawled into the room.

'What… what is that?' he screamed.

'That, sir,' I said calmly. 'That is your cure.'

The creature engulfed him.

A Letter from Maria

St Christophe
6th December 1783

Dear Mother,

The most horrible, terrible thing has happened! PLEASE come and get me! Oh, please do.

I had been looking for Monsieur Pond or Dr Smith to let them know where Amy was, and there was Monsieur Pond, standing on the veranda outside Dr Bloom's study. He was admiring the flowers.

'Ah, Maria, hello, your dress is very pretty,' he said, handing me a flower. He was dressed very smartly, I noticed.

'Why thank you,' I said, thinking him ever so nice. 'What are you doing out here?'

'Taking a stroll,' he answered after a pause. 'Yes, taking a perfectly innocent stroll. Does that sound reasonable? It's really quite true.'

I shook my head, smiling. 'And monsieur, what are you really doing?'

He stuck his hands in his pockets. 'I am waiting to see what happens. Softly, softly, catchee monkee. It can be our little secret.' He stopped, and stuck his tongue out as though he'd

just said something silly. 'Now then,' he said, his face stern.
'I heard a noise and some rustling in those bushes. Was that
you?'

I shook my head again.

'Oh dear,' he said. 'Well, far too big to be a rat. So… what is
it? And where has it gone?'

I was about to pluck up the courage to tell him about his
wife and Prince Boris when there came a sudden cry from
inside Dr Bloom's study. I felt Monsieur Pond's hand fall onto
my arm, but I was already running into the study, desperate
to stop any harm…

I fell through the French windows, and skidded to a halt…
What I saw was… Oh, Mother, I can't describe it, but I know
I've seen it before. It was just dreadful, and it seemed to fill
the entire room, and I screamed and screamed until Monsieur
Pond came in.

It took him only seconds, but by then everything was
normal. Monsieur Nevil was sitting on a chair, breathing
heavily, Dr Bloom was standing by the fire, looking cross, and
there was I, wilting under his thunderous gaze.

'What happened?' asked Monsieur Pond.

Dr Bloom managed a hearty laugh, and threw a hasty arm
around my shoulder. 'The poor child has had a fright, that's all.'

'It was in here! It was dreadful!' I protested, bursting into
tears. Oh, shameful behaviour, Mother, but I couldn't help it.

Monsieur Pond sank to his knees, staring me straight in the
eye. His voice was urgent, but quite gentle. 'Now then, Maria,
what was here? What did you see?'

'I can't say!' I cried, bursting into tears. I really, REALLY
couldn't.

Monsieur Pond looked around the room at the two men.
'Did you see? What was here? We both heard a cry.'

Monsieur Nevil, puffing and wheezing, just shook his head.

I could tell Dr Bloom was furiously cross, so cross I became even more frightened and started crying again.

I looked up at Monsieur Pond, desperate to tell him what I'd really seen, but I just couldn't.

Instead, he looked at me, so quiet and so kind. He sniffed the air. 'It smells funny in here,' he announced. Then he muttered, 'Warp transfer coil', almost to himself.

Horrible Madame Bloom appeared as if by magic, and took me back to my room, dragging me by my arm like a cheap governess. She washed the tears off my face with a flannel, scrubbing hard until it felt like she was tearing off my skin. 'Now then, Maria,' her voice was like stone, 'We do not like tell-tales and fibbers, do we?'

'But I saw it! I saw it!' I protested.

She reapplied the FREEZING flannel vigorously. 'What did you see, child? There was nothing to see!'

I stood, looking at her defiantly. I did not say anything. I just glared, using the look you employ whenever the dressmaker presents his bill.

Madame Bloom placed her hands on her hips. 'Very well, Maria. I can see there is no reasoning with you.' She sighed, as if she was hard-done-by and exasperated. I have never liked her, not since she refused to let me come home with you.

'Oh, my poor child,' she said. 'What are we going to do with you?' She pursed up her mouth and for an instant she looked truly sad.

'Let me go home!' I cried. 'Please, let me go home. I want my mother!'

Madame Bloom shook her head, smiling as she patted her hair into place. She checked her appearance in the mirror, and then smirked at me. It wasn't a nice smirk. 'No, Maria. I don't think so.'

With that she walked away, locking the door behind her. Oh, Mother, she will NEVER let me come home! I will NEVER see you, or the puppies. (Shall we call them Louis and Antoinette?)

I cried for a while, and then I started to fall asleep, staring miserably at the pillow. There was a quiet tap on the window. Who do you think was there? Why, it was Dr Smith!

'Hello, Maria!' he said, casually.

'But monsieur! However did you get up there? The ledge is very narrow and the ground is really such a long way away.'

He pulled a face. 'I'm suddenly very aware of that. You couldn't perhaps be an angel and let me in, could you?'

I ran to the window, and slid the casement up. He dropped in, landing on the carpet.

'Thank you,' he said, brushing stone dust from his knees.

'Did you climb up looking for me?' I asked.

He shook his head. 'That would be most improper. No, I was trying to find my patient. Amy. Have you seen her?'

The guilt showed on my face. I clapped my hands to my blushing cheeks. 'Monsieur Doctor, I am ever so sorry. I totally forgot! I tried to tell Monsieur Pond, but I got distracted. It was all ever so complicated. You see, I saw something terrible downstairs… I cannot say what, but they were doing something horrid to Monsieur Nevil.'

'What were they doing to him?'

'I cannot say,' I said, desperately. 'But please, monsieur, this is MOST important. I am trying to tell you about Amy. We were visiting the Prince in the Tower and I think the ogre captured him.'

'Ogre?' He blinked. 'Could you just repeat that a bit more slowly?'

I explained as best as I could about Prince Boris and his dreadful manservant Kosov and the chariot race. Twice.

Eventually Dr Smith stood up.

'Thank you, Maria. You've been very brave.'

I flushed with pride.

'But… I really think… you're in a lot of danger. More danger than a young girl should be in, no matter how brave she is.'

'It's all right, monsieur,' I said. Dr Smith made me feel all warm inside. He really is ever so kind. 'It really is going to be all right.'

He shook his head again. 'No, no it is not all right.' He stuck his hands in his pockets. 'Amy is missing, there's a secret patient under guard, the patients are being attacked, you can't go home, and there's something wrong about that beach… No, the time has come to tell you something very special.'

He looked at me very, very seriously.

'Right then. Maria. Please listen terribly carefully. If you ever get into trouble, I want you to scream this word at the top of your lungs. If I hear it, I will come running. All right?'

I nodded solemnly.

'Right. In a minute, I've got to go and rescue Amy. But first, promise me you'll stay safe.' He smiled, but he wasn't happy. 'Maria, I am going to tell you my secret name. It is very special. Can I trust you only to use it if you're in trouble?'

'Cross my heart.'

And so, Mother, Dr Smith told me his secret name. I'd love to tell you, but a promise is a promise.

Your ever loving

Maria

Dr Bloom's Journal

Drat the child. Drat that Maria!

If her mother won't have her, then… well, I don't see why I should. I've put up with her behaviour for quite long enough. But I won't stand for it. I just won't stand for it any longer. That's absolutely it. I am putting my foot down.

Perdita was very understanding. 'Of course you're right, my dear husband. Something must be done about Maria.'

'She nearly ruined everything with that fool Nevil,' I said, feeling the need to explain myself.

'But it's all fine now,' she said, soothingly.

She poured me a cup of tea, and I sipped at it gratefully. My Perdita makes wonderful tea.

'Don't worry. You can't cure everyone. In which case…' She smiled that beautiful, understanding smile of hers. 'We'll do something about the child tonight. We'll take care of her together.'

I crossed over to the window. In the darkness outside I could see Kosov walking down to the beach. 'Oh dear,' I sighed. 'I wonder what he'll tell them.'

Perdita clucked disapprovingly. 'I'm sure he'll just tell them the truth. It will be fine, my love, just fine. They are very understanding.'

She can always mollify me. But I am glad we're taking care of that wretched girl.

What Amy Remembered

No doubt about it, we'd been locked in by Prince Boris's servant. Which was a sackable offence, if you ask me.

Prince Dreamy was most apologetic, but far too calm about it for my taste. When he'd stopped coughing, that is. I offered him a glass of water, but he waved it away. 'Just… let… me… get… my… breath…' he pleaded.

While I waited I contemplated climbing out the window. Turns out it was a very big drop. So no.

'I guess it's just you and me, your majesty,' I muttered. 'I don't suppose you've got Connect 4?'

I was taking this quite casually, almost as though I was used to being locked up. I scratched away at my brain. What was my life like? Why couldn't I remember?

'What's Connect 4?' asked Boris. Good point. Turns out, that was another thing I couldn't remember. So I tried Pond Distraction Tactic No. 3, and changed the subject.

'How are you feeling?'

Boris sat up slightly. 'The fit has passed. Kosov is a saint, you know. If I hadn't have come here, if he wasn't looking after me… well, they said I'd be dead within a matter of months. The surgeons back at home had quite given up on me. And they were terrified of me! Certainly, I wouldn't have seen the spring. Instead, look at me!' He beat his chest proudly, only spoiling the effect with a tiny cough. 'It's amazing what a bit of fresh air will do, isn't it?'

'Isn't it?' I said, oddly unconvinced. He was supposed to be dying, wasn't he, and yet he was up and about after a couple of minutes. Sleeping Beauty was right – something was up with the Prince.

Boris had made us tea from a samovar before I'd realised. He was more like his old self. 'Don't fuss, dear Madame Pond,' he said. 'I'm quite better. The attacks are getting less and less severe. You really shouldn't worry. Some things are worth making an effort for, and one of them is tea.' He passed me a beautifully elaborate cup and saucer. 'Now, drink this and tell me all about yourself.' He smiled. It was a really charming smile.

So, I told him. Or, at least, as much as I could possibly remember. The more I said, the more scared I became as I realised there was really very little I knew about myself. I stopped.

The wind blew outside the window and the sea crashed against the rocks. The distant trees danced in the wind. It was like when you're little and there's one of those storms and you're really praying that no one is going to mention ghosts. We sat on Prince Boris's bed, sipping hot, sweet tea and looking at each other. He was terribly kind and he seemed to be listening attentively, even if he was yawning ever so politely. There was an odd expression in his eyes, as though, beneath all that merry laziness, he was calculating away intently, like a beardy computer.

I told him what I could about my boys and me – but it all sounded like nonsense. I could remember so very little. I knew we travelled a lot and that we did amazing things. There was something else – something dark and wrong that I couldn't quite remember. Oh, and I may also have told him that I quite fancied Dr Smith. Which in the 1780s was probably punishable by stoning or corsets.

'Poor Amy,' he said when I had finished. 'That was quite some bump on the head.'

I nodded. 'What's the matter with me?' I groaned.

Time passed. The wind blew, rattling the windows. We talked and drank tea. No Connect 4, but Boris found some draughts. Turns out draughts is a lot harder when you've not played it since you were a kid, and he beat me solidly. Several times.

'Oi,' I complained. 'You could let me win just the once. It would be chivalrous.'

Boris roared with laughter. 'I have told you, I am a Romanov and—'

'Yeah, yeah, you never let anyone win. Your wife must be *so* miserable.'

He shrugged. 'Madam Pond! We are locked up together! What care we of husbands and wives?'

I had a sudden worry – was I going to be found by my husband being chased round a bed by an excited member of the Russian Royal Family? Ah well, Ra Ra Rasputin...

But Boris's attention was elsewhere. He was checking the time on an elaborately jewelled carriage clock by his bedside. 'Where is Kosov?' he moaned. 'The man is late.'

'Does his majesty need his pillows plumping?' I asked. Truth to tell, I wasn't eager to meet the grumpy giant again.

Boris shook his head. 'No... no... it's not that...'

The storm crashed on. Something was wrong.

I looked out of the window. Through the rain-streaked

glass I could see… well, it looked like Maria, walking down to the beach. I hammered on the window. But she didn't hear me.

Boris hunted in the chest of drawers for cards. Then he stopped, and sank back onto the bed.

'Are you all right?' I asked. He was a very funny colour. By which I mean a very funny lack of colour.

'He doesn't normally leave me for so long…' Prince Boris gasped. He shook his head, as though drowning. 'Get Kosov… I need Kosov…'

He was a shadow of his cheerful self. I helped him back onto the pillows. 'I am so weak… please…' he muttered, sinking. And then he stared at me, aghast. 'Who are you?' he whispered. 'What are you doing in my room?'

Then the coughing started again.

I went and hammered on the door, called for a doctor, for my husband, for Kosov.

But no one came.

A LETTER FROM MARIA

St Christophe
6th December 1783

Dear Mother,

I know I promised not to go down to the beach again, but I couldn't help it, really I couldn't. After everything that has been going on, I just wanted to see what was happening down there.

The Dead were sat there, muttering and humming. The storm was raging around them, but they didn't seem at all bothered by it. I felt my heart leap into my throat as I crept up to them, but they didn't respond – they looked like they were frozen, waiting. They scared me. I tiptoed ever so gently away, and found Monsieur Pond.

'Hello, Maria,' he said softly and gently. 'How can I help you?'

'You are hiding behind a rock,' I said.

'Well, yes,' Monsieur Pond agreed sheepishly. 'There's room for one more.' He patted the cold sand next to him invitingly.

So I hid next to him. 'Why are we hiding?' I asked.

'Can it be our secret?'

Suddenly, Mother, everyone is telling me their secrets! I feel very proud. I told him, very seriously that he could trust me.

Why, Dr Smith had also told me a secret. Monsieur Pond did not look pleased at that.

'What did he tell you?' he asked sourly.

'Oh, monsieur,' I laughed. 'I am not to be tricked that easily!'

He said nothing. I stuck my tongue out at him.

He tried to ignore it, but eventually he smiled and pointed down to the sea. 'Maria, I am hiding because things are very wrong.'

'Right,' I said, very seriously. 'What have you seen, monsieur?'

Monsieur Pond started to roll his eyes like that schoolteacher we got rid of. 'Oh, Maria, Maria, I'm not sure I can even start to tell you everything that's wrong. Amy's ill, I'm not feeling myself at all, we're at a hospital that's about a hundred years early, it's the depths of winter and the patients are still sat on the beach in the middle of a storm...' He paused. Just then he sounded exactly like Dr Smith. Then his face fell. 'Oh, and there's a really very tall man standing behind you.'

I turned and squeaked. Kosov was towering over us.

A comforting hand seized mine. Monsieur Pond's. 'Now, don't be afraid,' he whispered, squeezing gently. He straightened, facing up to the giant. 'Good evening. My name is Pond.'

Kosov grunted at him.

'Russian, eh?' Monsieur Pond smiled. 'Well, there we go. Such fun.'

Kosov stepped closer. He grinned. It wasn't quite right somehow.

'Warp transfer coil,' said Monsieur Pond and then shook himself like a wet puppy. 'Sorry. I keep saying that, no idea why. What I meant was there's something wrong with your walk.'

Kosov paused.

'Well, when I say that, the posture's fine and all that. It's just that you're hovering about half an inch off the ground.'

I stared. Kosov, giant Kosov, was floating. Like a ghost. I screamed.

Kosov looked down at his feet and then back at Monsieur Pond.

'Made you look, ha-ha,' cried Monsieur Pond. His grip on my hand tightened. 'Let's run!' he cried.

We ran. Oh Mother, it was thrilling. Well, except that Kosov ran after us… or rather… flew. Like some ghost or a nightmare or something terrible, always just at our backs.

Somehow I felt utterly safe with Monsieur Pond. Very, very scared, but also very, very safe.

We ran through the mist towards the sea, Kosov seeming to run, or to glide behind us. We lost him for a moment in the mist, and then, I don't know, I twisted my foot, and lost my grip on Monsieur Pond's hand, and I was alone in the mist. I turned, but the mist was so thick! SO THICK!

I turned again, calling for Monsieur Pond. I could hear him calling me, and then suddenly, there in front of me was Kosov, his face like stone, making a grab for me.

I screamed and ran from him, falling back.

Suddenly I was in the sea, running into the waves.

'Maria!' I could hear Monsieur Pond shouting. 'Stay out of the water! Stay out of the water!'

'But monsieur!' I cried back to him, splashing along. 'It is very shallow! Where are you?'

He did not reply. I splashed on through the sea and the mist, my heart hammering in my throat.

Something grabbed my foot. At first I just thought it was the swell of the icy water.

Then it pulled, and I fell forward, face first into the freezing waves.

The pull increased, dragging me back and down.

I choked on a mouthful of freezing salt water, the waves breaking over my head and pushing me down. No, SOMETHING ELSE was pulling me down.

My left arm was grabbed, wrenching me further under. I could feel myself rushing through the water, feel it flying past in a bubbling rush. I was fighting for air, twisting over and over, down and down and down.

With a struggle, I broke the surface, wanting to scream but just coughing and choking, the sea still burning my throat and eyes. It all seemed so horribly familiar. Why is that?

The mist had cleared. I could still see the shore. I wasn't so very far away from land. I tried to fight towards it, but something was still dragging me back. Back and down. I couldn't move.

There on the shore, sat in their chairs, were the Dead. Watching me drown.

I called out to them, over and over.

But they did not move. They just carried on singing.

I felt so cold. So cold and so frightened.

I wondered – was now the time to call on Dr Smith? But how could Dr Smith help me? I got ready to scream out his secret name, but the salt water was still burning my throat and the words just WOULD NOT come out.

The mist pressed in around me, and the terrible thing in the water wrapped itself around me tightly and squeezed. As the breath rushed out of me, I was sucked under. My eyes were popping as the waves spread over my head…

Then a hand grabbed me. A warm, actual hand. And it pulled.

'Let her go!' I heard a voice say.

I opened my eyes. Again, it was wonderful Monsieur Pond. He was standing above me, his face stern as a statue, his hand tight around my wrist, pulling and pulling.

Around us the sea churned like a boiling stew. I could see things floating in it and a strange light dancing through it. For an instant it was almost like the waves drew back from us, and I could see all the way down to the wet sand.

Then Monsieur Pond held me tightly, his necktie tangling in my hair.

'I've got you, Maria,' he said. 'Come on.'

We waded through the thinning waves, reaching the shore.

There was Kosov. He was standing in front of us, arms folded.

'Hello again,' sighed Monsieur Pond.

Kosov nodded. 'You should have let The Sea have her,' he said.

'That was never going to happen.' Monsieur Pond sounded very firm.

Remember David and Goliath? Kosov looked so large, so fierce, and Monsieur Pond looked so small and so determined – like a tiny puppy facing up to a large wolf. For an instant he stood his ground and I thought he was going to stand and fight.

Then Kosov opened his mouth, and mist POURED out of it.

'Ooh, that's bad,' gasped Monsieur Pond. He grabbed my hand and we ran again.

We were nearly at the hotel, near the top of the cliffs.

We were both exhausted and panting, and soaked to the skin, the ice water freezing on our clothes.

But still Monsieur Pond struggled on, dragging us up and

up the stony path. Behind us, I knew, was Kosov, advancing like a golem.

The lights of the clinic looked so warm and friendly and so far away.

Monsieur Pond pushed me forward. 'Go inside, Maria,' he said. His face was sad and stern. 'I'll deal with… well, whatever that is, I'll deal with it. Find Amy. Keep running.'

I paused for a second, watching him turn around to confront Kosov, who was gliding up the stiff mountain path.

'Ah, good evening. Fancy meeting you…' And then Kosov's arms wrapped around Monsieur Pond in a great bear hug. Then he turned slightly, dangling Monsieur Pond over the cliff edge.

'I am warning you,' gasped Monsieur Pond, legs pedalling furiously at the air. 'I am an expert in … argh!'

Casually, Kosov let him go. Monsieur Pond vanished from sight. Kosov turned to me.

I screamed and ran, ran for the house.

Somehow, I made it to the door, running and crying. I slammed the door behind me and rested my weight against it, panting. The hallway was so dark I could see Kosov's shadow shining through the frosted glass. I wasn't even thinking about how I could possibly keep out such a brute. I was simply scared.

A hand rested on my shoulder. I looked up, gulping. It was Madame Bloom, staring emptily down at me, absently patting her hair in place with her free hand. Her other tightened its grip on my shoulder. She smiled.

'Good evening, Maria, my love. We have been ever so worried about you.'

A LETTER FROM MR NEVIL

St Christophe
6th December 1783

Octavius, my dear fellow!

Well, stop the clocks and blow me down with a feather! The cure is working. I have no idea how, but it's honestly miraculous. I feel so much better. I can almost run up stairs and (don't tell a soul here this) I can puff away on my pipe without feeling like it may be the last thing I'll ever do.

It's marvellous – I have only the haziest memories of the cure starting to work, but I tell you – tomorrow I am trotting down to the beach with the rest of them for more Fresh Sea Air.

I pottered into the lounge and caught myself whistling a jaunty little tune. The Glum Sisters were sat there – Helena and Olivia Elquitine, sawing away at some mournful ditty. They laid aside their instruments at my approach. Helena immediately began scribbling her wretched sums, while her busty sibling engaged me in polite conversation.

'You seem much improved, Mr Nevil,' Olivia ventured.

'Thank you, madam, you are too kind. You seem pale still.'

Oddly, I noticed myself flushing slightly when talking with her. Most unaccountable.

She demurred. 'It has been a while since I have received any treatment.'

'Ohhh,' I said, turning my face down. 'I had no idea that your case was so sadly advanced. You have my condolences, madam.' Bit of a facer, that. What do you say to a filly when she tells you she's coffin-bound? I regarded her, looking for signs of her imminent demise, and instead noticed for the first time that Olivia Elquitine was, well, a fine figure of a woman. Pale as porcelain.

Helena looked up from her scribbling and frowned, her face more pinched than ever.

'My sister,' began Olivia, looking embarrassed. 'She still receives treatment. But for some reason… my situation… I am afraid Dr Bloom hasn't selected me for the cure.' She coughed, and, for the first time I heard the tell-tale rattle. 'But he has been most kind.' She paused. 'Yes, most kind…'

I suddenly felt like a heel for gloating at my improvement. I laid a hand on hers, gently. 'Oh my dear,' I said, feeling a tenderness towards one worse off than myself. 'I am so sorry to hear that.'

'Thank you,' Olivia said and, for a moment, I detected more than simple politeness in her features. Odd woman. By candlelight she no longer looked quite so monstrously plump – instead she seemed rather pleasingly ample. I became acutely aware I was still holding her hand, and looked away, embarrassed.

We sat there in silence for a while, the only sound the scratching of her sister's pen as she worked on her sums.

I shall keep you updated on any further progress in my condition.

Your delighted servant,

Henry Nevil

WHAT AMY REMEMBERED

Prince Boris's door burst open. We were rescued!

'Did someone call for a doctor?' cried Dr Smith, staggering in. 'Sorry I'm late, shoulder-charging a locked door, actually a lot harder than it looks.' He winced, then looked around the room, heroic and mad, and then his eyes settled on me and lit up. 'Hello Amy! Oh, I am so pleased to see you.' And he hugged me, right there and then. 'Goodness me, you smell great.'

I could have kissed him. Actually I did, and then pulled back slightly. 'Careful, cheeky!' I protested. 'I have a husband.'

'Do you?' Dr Smith blinked, puzzled for a second. He regarded me, staring right into my eyes until I felt a little uncomfortable. 'Oh yes, I suppose you do.'

'So she keeps saying,' muttered Prince Boris from the bed.

'Tell me about it,' Dr Smith yawned and made yap-yap-yap gestures with his hand. 'He's a nice enough lad if you like your orange squash very weak.' He made a face, the rude boy, then turned to Boris. 'Hello! Who are you?'

Boris looked up and introduced himself.

'Great,' I thought. 'You boys can get to know each other and then have heaps of fun mocking my taste in men. Brilliant.'

I jabbed Dr Smith in the ribs, and indicated Prince Boris.

'Can you do anything for him?' I asked. 'He's very ill.'

'Is he now?' Dr Smith's tone was instantly fascinated. He peered into one of Boris's pupils intensely. 'Hum.'

He paused. It was one of those Simon-Cowell-before-a-result pauses.

He reached for something in his pocket, and used it to depress Prince Boris's tongue. 'Say ahh.'

'Ahhh,' said Prince Boris, winking at me.

'Right then,' said Dr Smith. 'Odd.' He pulled the thing out of Prince Boris's mouth, waving it around. 'Oh. Blimey. This is not a spatula. What is it?'

I stared at the stubby thing. It looked like the world's chunkiest novelty gift pen from Chessington World of Adventures. I coughed. 'That, Doctor, is the sonic screwdriver.'

'Ah,' Dr Smith boggled. 'Right. Is it? Oh dear.' Another pause. 'What does it do?'

'Well… it screws things… sonically. On a good day, we fight off monsters with it.'

'Monsters, eh?' Dr Smith nodded gravely and peered at it, as though seeing it for the first time. Then he pointed it at the doorway like a gun and said, hopefully, 'Pew! Pew! Pew!' He turned back to me. 'Like that?'

'Other way up,' I said, gently.

'Phoo.' Dr Smith plonked himself down next to me on Prince Boris's bed. 'Luckily, don't need a sonic anything to tell you the good news, Prince B. You are cured.'

'Very pleased to hear it, my dear sir.' Prince Boris smiled charmingly.

Dr Smith's face fell. 'Poor Amy here can barely walk, my brain is like scrambled egg, but oh ho, someone has cured you of tuberculosis. Sorry, not called that for about forty years.

But your wasting disease is wasting away. Quite remarkably you are getting better before my very eyes. That's wrong.'

'Wrong, sir?' Prince Boris smiled, but then his eyes shifted slightly.

'What is it?' I demanded. I know when a man is trying to hide something.

'Don't ask me how… but if I am getting better… it means that Kosov is coming.' Prince Boris looked alarmed.

'Who?' Dr Smith asked.

'Large, scary, goes grr!' I explained.

'Oh, met him.' Dr Smith waved the idea of him away. 'But you say that him being near you makes you better? Hmm…'

There was a sound from the doorway. Dr Bloom stood there, with Kosov next to him. 'Good evening, Dr Smith, Madame Pond. I see my door is broken,' purred Dr Bloom, his voice as silky as expensive shampoo. 'Now then, we don't want Prince Boris over-tiring, do we? Charming company is so very taxing, isn't it? I'm afraid we must ask you to let poor Prince Boris rest.'

'No need,' snapped Dr Smith. 'He is fine. Absolutely fine! I stake my reputation on it. And guess what… apparently his cure has got something to do with you, Mr Kosov.' He bounded off the bed, and stood on tiptoe, trying to glare eyeball to eyeball with him. He settled for squinting at Kosov's chin. 'Why is that, Mr Kosov? Would you care to explain?'

'No he wouldn't.' Dr Bloom shrugged. 'It's been a long day, and I have plenty of work still to do, Dr Smith. Come along, come along.' He ushered us to the door.

Prince Boris stood up, throwing off the covers. He immediately dominated the room, in the way that only a really posh person can. 'I think not, Dr Bloom,' he said. 'These people are under my personal protection.' He seemed more awake than normal. 'What are you planning to do with them?'

Dr Bloom sighed wearily. 'Kosov,' he commanded.

The giant manservant turned, ever so slightly, and glanced at the Prince. Puppet. Strings cut. Prince Boris fell back on the bed, blinking weakly.

Dr Bloom turned, sticking his hands in his pockets, and stared at us. 'Dr Smith and Madame Pond. I don't think either of you are very well. The time has come to find out what exactly is wrong with you.' He pulled something from his pocket, a rag that smelt of something really quite remarkable. I can tell you this because he immediately clapped it over my nose and mouth and it filled my brain with a reek like freshly mown grass and wax floors and cheap aftershave.

When I woke up, I was strapped to my wheelchair on the beach. It was night.

I was not alone. A little distance away from me were the empty deckchairs, flapping in the wind. The mist rolled in and around me. I could hear a voice on the sea air, like a song, chanting over and over again, not even a word, just a sound. The mist spread around me, the waves washed into the shore and out. It was freezing and I was very scared.

I tried moving, or getting up, or anything, but the more I struggled, the tighter the ropes holding me to the chair seemed to get. I remembered my lovely little old Dad trying to put up a deckchair on a family beach holiday. It had gone awfully wrong, and Mum said he'd been lucky not to lose a finger. It was that same feeling of helplessness.

Amy Pond. Sat on a beach, surrounded by fog. Come to think of it, fog that glowed, drifting in and out. And still that high-pitched singing noise echoing off the rocks, like the noise that opera singers make when they're trying to break glass. It was so cold. I was so scared. And I desperately wanted the Doctor to come and rescue me. I thought about just how much I needed him right now.

A little way out to sea, in the green-tinged darkness, a shape started to form. The shape of a man, walking out of the waves towards me…

Dr Bloom's Journal

6th December 1783

Dear, Dear, Dear, Dear Me.

Well, what a day. Still, all's well that ends well!

In good news, very good news, Kosov informed me that he had taken care of Mr Pond. We'd also made sure that his wife was safely on the beach, which would mean that we would shortly have everything we needed from her. And then she would trouble us no more.

This just left Maria and Dr Smith.

Perdita had tied them both up in my study. She had done her usual wonderful job of the knots and now stood behind my chair, her hands resting lightly on my shoulders. 'Tea, dear?' she asked, ever solicitous.

The little girl opened her eyes, looked around and starting crying.

'Now then, Maria, my dear,' I counselled her, using my best Dealing-Firmly-With-Children voice. 'Don't worry. Don't worry. We've brought you in for a spot more treatment. You remember the treatment, don't you?'

The girl nodded her head, but carried on staring at me, sobbing and calling for her mother.

My darling Perdita was at her side in an instant, wiping away the tears with a handkerchief and shushing her. 'There's nothing to be worried about, child, nothing at all,' she said, soothing her expertly.

Soon Maria was just sniffing and staring at me. 'What are you going to do to me?' she asked miserably. Very direct, that child. Well, not for much longer.

'Don't you worry about a thing. It'll be very quick and then it'll all be better, I can assure you.'

Maria turned in her chair, twisting around so that she could see Dr Smith, still dead to the world.

'Oh, he can't help you,' said my lovely wife firmly.

The ill-mannered little brat snapped at her, biting her on the arm. My lovely Perdita darted back, slapping at the wretch with her other hand. I ran to Perdita, pleased to see that she hadn't broken the skin. I glared at Maria.

'We have tolerated you for long enough, girl. You know that, don't you? Well, our indulgence comes to an end right now.'

I snapped my fingers and the French windows were flung open, the doors banging wide in the storm, wide enough to let what had been waiting outside flow in.

Maria started to scream.

'Oh yes, you remember it well enough now, don't you, my girl?' I snapped at her as it poured towards her. 'Believe me, it's as angry with you as I am. You have been a very naughty girl. Disobeying orders, and being quite uncontrollable. Well, we are bringing you to heel.'

The creature stopped before her chair and reared up over her, making a noise that was quite disagreeable.

Maria made some tiny little child pleading noises, but I haughtily ignored them.

Dear Perdita squeezed my shoulder. 'You are doing the right thing, my dear,' she assured me. 'Harden your heart, it's for the best.' She always knows exactly what to say.

'Goodbye, Maria,' I sneered, unable to resist the triumph. 'I'm afraid that with your usefulness over, it's time for absorption.'

The creature towered above her… Oh, how to describe it at this moment? Somewhere between smoke and pulsing green meat, as wet and cold as clay yet somehow as vital as lava. It looked incongruous, squeezed into the room between the settee and the fire. It looked wrong and yet magnificent. And it was about to solve the biggest problems in my world.

It paused – seeming to sniff the air. To sense the vastness it was about to sample. I remembered when Kosov first told me about the three strangers – that one of them contained great knowledge, great power. Something that The Sea could really, really use. Kosov was ever so excited. Now I was about to give The Sea what it really, really wanted. It had Mr Pond. It had Mrs Pond. Now I was going to give it Dr Smith.

The creature twitched. It was ready. I savoured the moment, and then gave the command. It began to descend.

Maria stopped snivelling, and stared up at it. She spoke quietly and firmly. I was astonished. 'Dr Smith…' she began, sniffing bravely. 'Dr Smith told me that if ever I was in trouble, and if ever I needed him, *really* needed him, I was to use his secret name. He said it was incredibly powerful and I could use it to defeat you.'

'Go on, child,' I laughed. 'A name cannot help you.'

'Yes, yes it can,' she said, babbling excitedly. 'Because Dr Smith is the most wonderful man in the whole world. And his secret name is all I need.'

'Enough!' I cried. 'Absorb her!'

Maria, the vile little brat, stared up at the creature, threw open her mouth and screamed like only a child can. She yelled out one word…

'*Rory!*'

WHAT DR SMITH THOUGHT

I am the Doctor.

I am in a room. The room is very large and very dark. In the middle of the room is a small box that's even blacker. With 'THIS WAY UP', 'HANDLE WITH CARE' and 'DO NOT OPEN TILL CHRISTMAS' chalked on it.

It is time to open the box. It is time to begin again.

I open the box.

Oh.

I am not the Doctor after all.

Begin again.

A Letter from Maria

St Christophe
6th December 1783

Dear Mother,

It worked! I called out Dr Smith's secret name, and he woke up, all startled like he'd sat on a pincushion. He saw the THING that was hovering over me and squealed, pressing himself back against his chair and howling. It wasn't exactly the bravery I was hoping for, but I could kind of see his point. Whatever it was, it looked dreadful and smelt worse. And it was coming for us.

'Rory!' I yelled again. 'Your name is Rory!'

His head snapped round and he stared at me. 'What?' he said. Then he licked his lips. 'Right. Right. Yeah…' He blinked. 'That makes sense.' He nodded casually and, somehow ignoring the giant monster, turned back to Dr Bloom. 'Yes, that's it,' he said. 'My name is Rory Williams.'

The Blooms looked at him.

'I… I'm sorry, but I don't understand,' said Dr Bloom. He sounded different. Worried.

'Neither do I,' explained the man called Rory. 'But I'm not the Doctor. You think you've won, but you haven't. You've got

87

the wrong man.' He laughed then, a laugh that turned into a cough.

'What?' Dr Bloom cried. It was odd, Mother, it was like everything in the room had changed without anyone moving a muscle.

Dr Smith… well, *Mr Rory Williams* looked at Dr Bloom and really, really smiled at him. It took quite the hero to be tied to a chair and be winning. And Rory was my hero. You remember that maid who broke things and denied it so impudently? That was the same expression that Rory wore, tied down firmly to the chair, but so triumphant.

'You've got the booby prize,' he taunted Dr Bloom. 'The Doctor is still out there somewhere and he's now got his memory back. You've just got me tied to a chair. I'm pretty worthless. Sorry.' He managed to shrug despite being tied up, clearly a practised manoeuvre. 'Really. I honestly don't know why I've been pretending to be him, but I am definitely not him. I am plain, simple Rory Williams from Leadworth. It's a lovely English village with a post office and a duck pond,' he added, helpfully. He smiled, clearly pleased with himself.

His smirk faded as he noticed the creature again. He narrowed his eyes. 'Sorry if I'm pointing out the obvious, Dr Bloom, but you're a nasty piece of work. I mean, you've got me tied up next to a little girl. And is that thing really going to eat us?' He wrinkled his nose and turned to me. 'You know, I should be used to this kind of thing by now, but I'm really not.' He seemed different, Mother. Less… odd, less like a schoolteacher, more… friendly and fun and somehow charming. He pointed at the towering creature with his shoulder. He winked. 'Now then, Maria, don't you worry about that thing, the Doctor will probably be crashing through that door in a second.'

'The Doctor?' demanded Dr Bloom. 'Who is this heroic Doctor you're going on about?'

'Ah,' said Rory, visibly growing. 'Bit taller than me, bit weirder, goes crashing around, breaking things. Always rescuing me at the last moment.' He coughed and repeated loudly: 'At the last moment.' His eyes wandered over to the door, and for a second he looked hopeful.

'Did he by any chance wear a bow tie?' I asked, suddenly fearful.

'Yes,' he said. 'Looks silly, doesn't it? Why?'

'I think he may be dead,' I said.

'Quite right.' Dr Bloom laughed like a drunk uncle. 'Kosov threw him off a cliff.'

'Oh,' said Rory. He seemed crushed. The moment of triumph had passed. I felt so sorry for him, but also disappointed – I'd used the secret word and very little seemed to have happened.

He went silent for a moment, then he looked up. There was a different tone in his voice. Worried. Defensive. Really angry. 'Where's Amy?'

Dr Bloom leaned back against his desk. 'She is down on the beach,' he admitted eventually.

'Oh.' Rory thought about this. 'That is not good,' he said, really angry.

'Not good at all.' Dr Bloom nodded in agreement. 'So you see, my dear sir, you've not won anything at all, have you?'

What Amy Remembered

I sat in my chair on the beach, watching the figure come striding out of the fog towards me. It was so cold, and I could hear the distant singing from the sea.

The figure walked through the waves, each footstep making a churning noise as it pushed against the churning sea. The mist rolled across, hiding it from sight for a second. The fog was all around, almost choking me. I was breathing it and it felt thick – like cold soup. Cold soup that glowed. I tried not to breathe it in, choking on it. I realised that the fog itself was making the strange whispering, singing noise – like it was calling my name.

Amy, Amy, Amy, Amy… over and over.

I couldn't see anything, not even my own feet – just this cold green glow. I have never felt so alone. I missed… my husband. I missed… the Doctor… I missed my boys so much.

Something moved and shifted in my brain, like the singing buzz along a railway line before a train turns up. Something important was coming. Something was clicking into place.

I was almost blind and alone and I could hear something walking towards me… *Slap! Slap!* of wet footsteps on the beach. In a panic, I grabbed at the bath chair, turning it somehow, desperately tugging at the wheels and trying to drag it into life, to get me away – but the wheels were stuck in the sand. But the more I struggled, the looser I could feel my bonds getting – perhaps, just perhaps, I could get free if I tipped the chair.

I started to rock the chair backwards and forwards, all the while hearing those footsteps, expecting an arm to shoot out from the mist and grab me. But finally, with a crash, I went down, head-over-heels, shooting out of the chair like a brilliant failure of the Scottish Space Programme.

I landed on the wet sand with a firm thud and tried to stand up – but my legs were still too weak to take any notice of me. Try as I might. I also couldn't see which way to go – disoriented, I realised even the wheelchair had vanished in the fog. I was crawling on my hands and knees in wet sand, utterly lost.

Then I looked up, and I saw him. The mist had cleared slightly. And there, yards ahead of me, like a hero on a little rocky outcrop stood... It was definitely him – I'd have known that silhouette anywhere.

Oh.

Like an elastic band pinging my ear, I felt a sharp stinging sensation, and realised it was my head. Someone had flicked a switch in it, and it had started working. Like a box of missing information had suddenly opened. My brain suddenly sorted itself out like a jigsaw puzzle, everything falling into place, including the missing bit of sky tucked down the back of the sofa. I realised everything that had gone wrong. Everything that I had forgotten the last time I was on this beach. I knew who was standing on the rocks by the sea.

The Doctor.

I crawled towards him, crying with relief, calling his name

over and over. He meant so much to me. My Doctor. The man I…

He started to turn towards me and then… something crashed out of the mist behind him, carrying both shapes into the sea. I screamed, trying to stand, but nothing. I was left crouched on the beach, crying and alone and helpless. I beat my fists in the sand, but that didn't do anything.

When I stopped, I realised something.

Slap! Slap!

Footsteps, coming nearer.

The Doctor had come back, and something had killed him. Something dreadful that was now coming for me.

Madly, I crawled towards the sea, calling out the Doctor's name, in case he'd survived and was somewhere out there. The waves started to rush around me, freezing cold running over my hands and legs, dragging at my clothes. The fog started to push down on me. And those footsteps were still coming, closer and closer.

I had no idea what to do next. I struggled desperately to my feet and, of course, immediately fell. As I tumbled, a cold hand gripped my wrist like steel. I cried out in pain and stared up – a man was standing over me in the mist.

It looked like the Doctor. But I knew. I knew… It wasn't. And then, when it spoke to me with that flat, dead voice, I was certain.

'Amy Pond,' it said, cautiously, as though trying the name out for the first time. 'I've come back for you…'

A Letter from Maria

St Christophe
6th December 1783

Dear Mother,

Things looked bad. Really bad. Just AWFUL, and I felt ever so let down. I had been hoping that my hero would rescue me like a storybook princess from a castle. Instead we were still tied to chairs. Rory wasn't the man I'd thought him to be. He was nice, but he was no hero. And above us – that strange cloud of... No, I just can't describe it. It's too horrible. But it was starting to pour, very slowly, down towards us.

'Think of something,' I hissed at him.

'I've got nothing,' Rory said with a shrug.

Dr Bloom was watching, quietly amused. His wife was pottering around, actually tidying the study. As though seeing us being eaten alive was boring her. I never liked her, Mother, and now you know why. She was fussing as she arranged Dr Bloom's pens neatly in order.

'Pens,' muttered Rory.

'Monsieur?'

'Could you reach my left pocket?' he asked.

I managed to twist around in my chair, my hand grabbing

something pen-like sticking out of Rory's pocket.

'Very good,' said Rory. He winked at me. 'Now… point it at THAT. No. Other end, apparently.'

Well, I had no idea what it did, but I knew which end to push. I hoped it was not a gun. It had a very pretty light at one end. Maybe that would distract everyone.

Instead it pumped out a sound… a sound so horrifying I squealed.

So did the creature above us, reeling back.

'Oh, well done, Maria,' cried Rory over the din.

'What are you doing?' gasped Dr Bloom. He ran to his wife. She was doubled over in agony. It looked like whatever I'd done was really, really hurting her. Good.

Rory stood up with some difficulty, the chair still tied to him. He leaned over me and managed to pull my ropes free. Then he turned to Dr Bloom.

'We're escaping,' he said. 'Goodbye.' Chair still tied to his back, he ran with me from the room.

I take it all back. Rory is just wonderful.

Your ever loving

Maria

Dr Bloom's Journal

Oh, for the sake of Saint Peter! What a disaster!

One of the strangers and the child Maria have escaped.

I watched them go. 'No! Stop!' I cried, running to the door. 'Stop! Stop! Stop!'

Then I realised I was shouting at no one, and I felt silly.

Her own pain overcome, my beloved Perdita was at my side in an instant, soothing me. 'I've rung for help,' she said. 'They can't get far.'

I looked up at her. 'Are you sure?'

She nodded. 'I will go and issue instructions.'

She left the room with a swish of skirts.

That left me alone with the Thing. It stood there, patiently. Waiting for orders. So, with a weary sigh, I sent it away. Off it went back down to The Sea.

Dear Perdita came back in, closing the French windows after it. She tidied her hair and paused before turning to me, her face sympathetic. 'Don't worry, my darling. It's all in hand. Why not have a rest now? It will all be better in the morning.'

And it will be. Because she tells me so.

*

7th December 1783

A new day! A glorious new day!

Well, I say that. It was perishing cold, the water in my bedside basin nearly frozen, and even the carpet chilly. The maid had lit the fire in my bedroom, but the heat was hardly spreading out beyond the hearth.

Perdita had dressed already and had an excited look on her face. 'Come, my dear, come and see.'

It was the same look my mother wore when she told me the brilliant news that it had snowed. The sight was almost as wonderful.

I stood at my study window and watched as the patients were wheeled out onto the veranda and down the sea path to the beach. Each one, still and silent, bumped along in their chair, their ever-faithful attendants with them.

I felt Perdita squeeze my hand. 'Look,' she breathed.

And then I saw her. The girl with the bright red hair, slumped in her chair, staring blankly ahead of her, being wheeled patiently along. Miss Pond, and the figure behind her, grim and expressionless, a man I now knew was called the Doctor. Only it wasn't really the Doctor. This version of him had come from The Sea, to learn all it could about Amy Pond. She was completely in its control.

'What a wonderful day!' I beamed. I actually beamed.

'Exactly,' Perdita agreed, clasping my hand to her lips. 'Oh beloved! It is taking her down to the beach. Soon we will know everything about them.'

I left my study, and crept out behind our guests, following at a distance, trying not to rub my hands with glee. I felt the same childish thrill I always felt as the wet sand sank under my feet, leaving squelching footprints. I remembered that first time I had stood on the beach and realised there was something there, something in the water that called to me, that rolled out of the mist and into my mind, wrapping itself around my every thought and giving me everything that I wanted. Ever since, I'd always kept at a wary distance as the spirits worked their magic on my patients – every single day they came down to the shore, and they left better. I don't know how it works, but I know that it does. The Sea gives them exactly what they need. And in return… it learned all about them.

It wanted Madame Amelia Pond, I knew that. It had tried before, and it had failed, summoning Kosov to bring them to me. There was something about those three strangers – how had they come here? What were they? Something I did not know and The Sea wasn't telling me. But it wanted desperately to try again.

Now it had its chance. It did not matter about the boy called Rory. It was a pity about the man called Doctor. The real Doctor was probably lost on the waves and would wash up in a fisherman's net somewhere.

But Amy Pond. Oh! The Sea had briefly been able to touch her mind – it knew that the Doctor was the most important thing in the world to her, and it had given a copy of him to her. If they spent enough time together, the copy would become every bit as good as the real Doctor. It stood there now, wheeling her down to the beach, one hand resting lightly on her shoulders, drawing all it could from her.

There she sat, her head nodding slightly, those pretty eyes wide open, listening to The Sea as it washed in, waves folding over and over, calling out *forget, forget, forget* as it washed across the beach. Her hair was the brightest thing in the world that morning, red against all that grey. Her skin was so pale, pale as a freshly laundered sheet. She was probably cold, but she wouldn't feel it – not as The Sea reached into her.

I watched as the fog came up from The Sea, rolling out along the beach, little fingers stretching up across the beach, and dancing around her feet. The fog glowed slightly, a faint green, as if thousands and thousands of little candles flickered inside it.

It would not be long now before it knew everything it needed.

The figure of the Doctor stood behind Amy Pond, his hands resting on her shoulder. Gentle, but firm. There was no escape for her. Not any more. Soon she would remember, and then everything of hers would belong to us.

WHAT AMY FORGOT

So the TARDIS had crashed, and there we were on a beach, spilling out of the blue box in a dazzled heap.

Rory and I were just glad to be alive, but the Doctor was already bounding around as excitedly as a dog chasing after a rubber ball. His sonic screwdriver was held out in front of him, lighting up the night like a torch.

'We've arrived!' he boomed, then repeated the phrase, testing the echo. 'Côte d'Azure, lovely spot for a holiday but not in... ooh, early December. 1780s. Just around the corner from the French Revolution. Not perhaps the best time for topping up the tan and reading John Grisham. But hey, what do I know? Suit yourself. There's beach towels aplenty in a trunk somewhere in the TARDIS and... Ow!'

The Doctor stopped and stood very, very still.

We caught up with him. We hadn't been badly injured by the crash, even though the TARDIS now lay on its side, door open, light spilling out of it weakly. Rory was rubbing a bruised elbow.

'It's Baltic,' I said, huddling closer to Rory for warmth. 'It is absolutely freezing.' Then I realised the Doctor had stopped moving. 'Are you OK? Doctor?'

'Ow, sorry.' The Doctor spun round on the spot, facing us. 'Sorry. Ow. Something out there. Tiny little psychic probe, tugging away at my head. Reading my mind. Which it Must Not Do! Bad Psychic Thing!' The Doctor flapped a hand. 'Get out, get out, get out!' He grinned, tapping his forehead. 'I've got expert mental shielding. But ooh, it's having quite a go.' He threw the sonic screwdriver to Rory, who just about caught it, bless him. 'Torch setting, see if you can see anything. I can't move at the moment. Due to... ouch.' The Doctor winced. 'If that's you again, Derren Brown, show yourself, you bad boy.'

'Is that what brought us here?' asked Rory, casting about the beach with the sonic screwdriver. All I could see was sand and rocks, sea and fog.

'Um, possibly.' The Doctor frowned. 'Something alien and a bit wrong twinkling away in space-time. The old girl couldn't resist that and... Oh dear.'

'Warp transfer coil,' said Rory.

The Doctor's face fell. 'I was afraid you'd say that. Naughty psychic thing, still jabbing away. Causing a bit of brain spillage.' He tapped Rory on the forehead. 'Sorry about that. If it's any consolation I now know that you really don't like kippers. Who does?' He screwed up his face. 'Stop that! Stop that at once! My name is the Doctor and I can help you if only you... stop...'

'... If only you stop reading my mind,' said Rory. 'Keep out. Beware of the Dog. Here there be dragons.'

'Rory?' I grabbed him. 'Are you OK?'

'Dangerous.' Rory's head spun to face me, but his expression was very odd. 'Amy Pond,' he spoke, his voice all wrong. 'Something very bad is about to happen. Very bad and a bit painful. Run.'

'I'm not leaving you.' I was firm. 'Either of you.'

'Get back to the TARDIS, please…' begged Rory, as the Doctor's hand jerked out, pointing. 'Quickly now, hurry up, bits of brain going everywhere. Get out of the way. Doing what I can. That thing is less of a mind probe, more of a food processor.'

'Whizz,' said the Doctor. He sank down to his knees, his feet drumming on the sand.

Rory's face twisted, his voice buckling. 'He's right, Amy. I don't know what's happening, but it really hurts. Please. Keep back. I love you… Whizz.'

And Rory fell over, his legs twitching.

I ran.

Sorry. I left them. I didn't know what else to do.

I ran, ran as fast as I could towards the TARDIS. Maybe there'd be something in there that could help me. All around me was a fog, a fog that danced with strange lights and pushed at my head. The TARDIS wasn't much further. I kept running. I could see the door up ahead. Just keep running, Amy, just keep them out of your head, get inside, work out what to do. Save Rory. Save the Doctor.

The TARDIS door slammed shut, trapping me outside. In the dark on the beach, the only light was that strange glowing mist all around me, pressing in.

I heard a voice in my head. A voice that could only be the Doctor's. 'Sorry, Amy,' it whispered, and I felt my knees give way.

I lay there for a bit. One of three bodies lying on a beach as the mist rolled around us.

Then my brain switched off.

WHAT AMY REMEMBERED

My brain switched back on.

'Watch,' whispered the Doctor's voice in my ear.

Figures came from the sea. From the mist. I couldn't quite see how – but it's not like they bobbed up from underwater. They just coalesced, striding forward, becoming more and more solid. Just a shadow, then a silhouette, then, as it reached the shore, a fully formed person, clothes and all. Some of the figures were old, some young, there were children and, in one case, a dog. They stepped out of the sea utterly dry and they walked up to the patients. The mist fell away from them as they stepped across the sand, leaving no footprints at first, and then gradually they settled into the ground, solid and real.

The poor patients, each one still and almost lifeless, each one suddenly faced by a figure, looming over them. The strange singing note drifted out from the water, keeping time with the waves. An old man looked up from his chair as a tiny fat lady danced up to him, taking his hand in hers. She smiled at him, and he smiled back at her then stood up. They started, ever so gently, to dance.

A tired-looking woman with grey hair laughed as her hands

were seized by two children, two silently laughing children who dragged her into the dance.

There was fat Mr Nevil, slumped snoring under a rug. Even comatose he looked sour. Until a big dog with a shiny wet nose laid its muzzle in his lap and tapped him with a paw, looking up at him with big beggy eyes. And then Mr Nevil stood up, beaming like it was Christmas, and he started to dance with the dog. It was a little awkward, but they were doing it.

'Fascinating,' breathed the figure of the Doctor in my ear. I could feel the hairs on the back of my neck prickling. 'Shall we dance?' he muttered.

'Must we?' I asked him. But I gave him my hand and we danced on the beach, stiff and awkward. I noticed my legs were working again. I wondered if that was his doing.

'Are you real?' I whispered.

'Are you?' he countered.

Then he trod on my foot and I knew he was real.

'Sorry.' The Doctor frowned. 'Always getting born with two left feet.'

I sighed. 'So what's the plan?'

'Well, first I convince you that I'm real, then I win your confidence, and finally the mind parasite out there devours your brain.'

'Oh great.' I smiled. 'Thanks for being honest.'

'Not a problem.' He winked. 'Don't worry, I'm shielding you. When we crashed here and it first attacked me, I was caught with my mental trousers down. Not any more. Psychic force field's intact. Belt and braces. Braces, by the way, are very cool.' He tapped his head. 'I've put a brick wall round your brain, Pond. Nothing can get through.'

'Won't whatever it is out there be suspicious?'

'Well, in a bit, maybe. But I've put you in a trance for hours, and while you were asleep I've scattered some false little Amy Pond brainwaves all around the barrier. Lots of lovely memories of holidays bird-watching on the Isle of Man.'

'I've never been to the Isle of Man,' I hissed.

'Well there we are, the perfect crime. I was improvising.' The Doctor flashed a reassuring smile. 'It'll take the parasite a while to realise that it's just getting a few holiday snapshots of the Greater Crested Glebe and nothing juicy. Not a whisker of the real Amy Pond, the little girl who has travelled through universes. And absolutely nothing about her friend the Doctor. No. It absolutely mustn't read my mind.' The Doctor's voice was very firm. 'Now I'm myself again. Took me quite a while. Luckily someone threw me off a cliff last night and things jogged back into place on the way down. Result! When I came to, I was pretty much myself again. Not too sure about the colour puce, mind, but it'll come back, eventually. Anyway, pretty much normal service, just in time to stop that thing out there fooling you by sending in the clones. Knocked its copy of me out into the sea and came and rescued you. It's all good.'

'What about Rory?' I asked. This was very important.

'Oh, he's back to normal,' the Doctor said. 'Lots of my memories ended up in his head – lots of spare room in there. Bit of a rushed job. Not my finest work, but bits of brain were flying everywhere. I had to move my mind in a hurry – and let's face it, Rory Williams is the last place anyone would look.'

I glowered at him. Sometimes he can be SO rude. I stamped on his foot and he winced.

'Sorry. Anyway, he's fine now – all my memories have snapped back. Still missing my favourite chutney recipe. New fact – that boy really does hate kippers. Which is annoying because I really fancy one now.'

'Enough kippers.' I prodded him, gently continuing to waltz to the ethereal singing. 'What are we up against? An alien version of *Strictly Come Dancing*?'

'Oh, Amy Pond, you are absolutely my favourite,' sighed the Doctor. 'Look at our fellow patients. About three minutes ago, each and every one was dying of a dreadful, incurable disease. Now look at them. They're dancing!'

I looked. Even grumpy Mr Nevil looked years younger and happier.

'The brain parasite out there gives them someone they love. A little bit of itself that they trust enough to let it wrap around them and heal them.'

'Aw,' I said. 'That's quite nice.'

The Doctor's face stopped me.

'Isn't it?'

'No, Amelia, it is very wrong indeed.'

As we stood there, surrounded by the dancing dead, he told me why. It was utterly terrifying.

A Letter from Maria

Dear Mother,

Oh, what a wonderful night! It was like the best game of hide and seek – you remember for my seventh birthday party when all my friends came and we hunted over the entire house and then had meringues?

It was like that. Only without meringues. And a little bit scary.

Monsieur Rory Williams and I were being hunted throughout Dr Bloom's clinic. We hid in cupboards, under beds, in a cellar, and even, at one tense moment, under the desk in Dr Bloom's study.

It was when we were there, curled up in a ball, that I whispered to Rory, 'Sir, what do you think will happen when they find us?'

Rory shook his head sadly, his voice even quieter than mine. 'I don't know. Nothing very good. I'm not exactly lucky.'

'What was that creature we saw last night?'

'I have absolutely no idea.'

'I have seen something like it before,' I told him. And I had,

I just cannot remember how or why. But I know it was here. Oh Mother, when you get this, can you try and remember for me? If you can, do write back and tell me. I know I am sending you ever so many letters at the moment, but this is the most EXCITING time of my whole life.

We spent some of the night in the kitchen. I ate some cheese and two slices of cake. Rory did not eat. We heard a squeaking of wheels, and we looked through to where Amy was being wheeled stiffly past by a man who I had thought was Monsieur Pond, but Rory put me right.

'That is my wife,' he said, sounding ever so sad. 'And the man with her is the Doctor. And they're just not right.'

'Should we go to them?'

Rory shook his head and slumped down on Cook's chair. 'Something is very wrong. I want to. But I can hear the Doctor's voice in my head, telling me not to.'

'How?'

'I don't know. But it's what's had me so confused these last couple of days. I think I ended up with some of him in my head.' He grimaced, like he was swallowing cough medicine.

I nodded. Amy, Rory and the Doctor. Three wonderful and marvellous people who have such extraordinary lives. Oh, Mother, when I come home, do you think we can have them to stay?

So the two of us sat in the kitchen until the restaurant was empty, then we went and hid under a table. 'We'll just stay here and think of something.'

We stayed there for hours. I think I even slept a bit. I know Monsieur Rory snored gently. But after a while, breakfast came and went, and we were alone. I wondered if we should move out… but Rory wanted to make sure we were absolutely alone.

He was right to worry.

'Monsieur,' I breathed. 'Someone is coming!'

I could hear my heart pounding ever so loudly. Rory stared at me. We could hear footsteps coming closer and closer. We were about to be discovered. My heart leapt into my mouth!

The footsteps stopped at our table!

They paused!

Oh, Mother!

They crouched down!

They lifted back the tablecloth.

'Rory! Maria!' cried Amy. 'I am so pleased to see you.'

Then another face appeared. The Doctor. He grabbed hold of Rory's ankle, dragging him protesting out from under the table. 'Rory!' he grinned, wrapping him in an enormous bear hug that squeezed the breath out of him. 'I've been you!'

'Right,' mumbled Rory.

'You've had a gorgeous time, I bet.'

'Not… especially, no.'

The Doctor stepped back, his eyes were wide and dancing. 'Did you escape from any monsters? Did you set anything on fire? I'm always doing that. Honestly, one minute it's Tell Me Your Plans, the next it's BOOOM! My insurance premiums are terrible.' The Doctor uses ever such strange words. 'Anyhow, you're all back to normal, yes?'

'Yes.' Rory was ever so tight-lipped.

The Doctor nudged him with his elbow. 'Go on then. What was it like being me? Wasn't it just a bit brilliant? Did it open up your tiny mind?'

Rory looked a little ill. 'It's nice to be me, actually. I'm not a hero.'

'Oh, don't be modest. You've done some wonderful things.' The Doctor winked at me. 'You've married Amelia Pond and can probably mend a fuse. I've never got the hang of that. Very important.' He turned to me and lowered his voice. 'It's OK, Maria, you don't need to know what a fuse is. They're rubbish.' He turned back to Rory. 'Anyway, Rory, you've got your brain back…'

Rory sat on the chair and looked up at the Doctor. For a second he looked angry. 'And what was it like being me?' he asked.

The Doctor tugged at his braces, embarrassed. 'Oh, don't apologise – I'm sure I'll get over it.' He waved it away.

At which point, Amy reached down and took my hand. 'Come along, Maria, let's go find some buns. They'll probably be shouting at each other for a bit.'

Your ever loving

Maria

A Letter from Mr Nevil

St Christophe

7th December 1783

Dear Octavius,

I had an early breakfast with Olivia Elquitine.

'Aren't you going to play your violin?' I asked her, chewing on a pastry (actually, one can get used to those things).

She shook her head, smiling. 'We never play in the mornings. And my sister doesn't come down to breakfast. She prefers to sit in her room.'

'What does she do?' I asked. 'What are all those figures she's always scribbling? Dressmaker's bills?'

Again, Olivia smiled at me. 'My sister is quite brilliant with mathematics, Mr Nevil.'

'To be sure, to be sure,' I ventured, humouring her, but she was having none of it. There followed a quite exhausting explanation of logarithms and whatnot, but I merely nodded away, all the while thinking that Olivia would look rather good as the mistress of the hunt back home, perched on a horse, leading a charge.

I was aware of a tap at my shoulder. It was Mrs Bloom, all silky charm.

'Time for your morning treatment, Mr Nevil,' she oozed.

I glanced at Olivia and noticed her frown. 'My dear Mrs Bloom,' I protested. 'Perhaps… well, perhaps I can postpone?'

Mrs Bloom shook a firm negative. 'Come along now, I really do insist.'

'Ah, well, in that case, perhaps I should…' I stood up and bowed to Olivia, carefully avoiding her glare.

As I set off for the beach, I could see the damn filly looking at me. She seemed disappointed.

Ah well, that's women for you! I'm sure she'll keep.

Your servant,

Henry Nevil

What Amy Remembered

Never take the Doctor for granted. Just when you think you know where life is going, you're having breakfast with a Russian prince. Once the Doctor and Rory had stopped arguing, the Doctor insisted we go and hide in Prince Boris's rooms.

Prince Boris was only too happy to see us. 'Ach! I love refugees!' he said. 'My mother once took in a whole group of gypsies for months on one of her dacha. Said it was good luck for the hens. And you two gentlemen travel under false identities! How daring! More caviar?'

Yes, that's right – we had caviar for breakfast. To be honest, it was a little bit like when someone sticks too much anchovy on a pizza. Although the Doctor was layering it with marmalade and swore it was heavenly.

Rory seemed relieved to be back to his normal self, perched on the bed, drinking tea, while the Doctor tried to make amends.

'Sorry about messing with your head, Rory. It was a bit of an emergency.'

'That's fine,' said Rory politely. 'Everything's back now…'

'Well, almost,' muttered the Doctor. 'I don't suppose you can remember…'

'Yeah, there's a recipe for Onion Chutney that I really think isn't mine.'

'Thank you!' The Doctor hugged him warmly. 'I have missed that!'

'I'm fine thanks, by the way,' Rory muttered. 'All back to normal.'

He'd need a bit of tender loving care and a back rub later, I could just tell. Meanwhile… well, breakfast.

But even then, Rory wasn't at ease. 'Where's your pet ogre?'

'Kosov?' Boris shrugged. 'Out and about, my friends, probably looking for you, eh?' And he laughed. I noticed there was no rattling echo when he laughed now. He seemed much better, the picture of health. Bit like George Clooney doing Rasputin, frankly. He was even wearing a tasselled velvet nightcap that I noticed the Doctor eyeing up. If Boris didn't watch out, that'd go missing and we'd never hear the last of 'Nightcaps are cool'.

While Boris made coffee as hot and thick as lava, the Doctor explained the situation to us all, scribbling the odd note on the window with a sharpie. Little Maria sat in the corner, licking stray caviar from her fingertips and staring at him with wide-eyed admiration. He does that to girls and never notices. Not once.

'So, basically – turns out, we're time travellers. If the universe has a problem and no one else can help, then it's us. The A-Team. The Doctor and the brilliant Amy Pond.' Rory coughed, quietly. 'Oh yeah, and Amy's husband, Roger.'

'Rory.'

'Whatever.'

Maria let out an admiring gasp.

Boris was nodding sagely. 'So you come from the future?' he asked.

The Doctor nodded. 'Sometimes the future, sometimes the past, and sometimes just a little to the right. That's us.'

'And what's wrong with this place to make you come here?' Boris asked sternly.

'I have been dying for someone to ask me that!' the Doctor beamed at him, delighted, and that's when the lecture began. One day, I swear he'll do a PowerPoint. 'Right then. Let's just for a moment ignore the utterly mad aliens on the beach –' Boris opened his mouth, but the Doctor sailed on, bless him. 'I said ignore them! Not one word! Fact. We are in one of the most important years in history. 1782!'

'1783,' whispered Maria.

'What I said! 1783. Very, very important year. Well, not that much happens, actually, but it's just around the corner from a whole lot of interesting. Wars, revolutions and so on all over Europe – the kind of grim human thing you lot do so well.'

'I take it you are here to prevent that?' Boris looked grave. To be fair, he'd taken the whole 'we're from the future, hello' thing remarkably well. He looked vaguely bored by it, but then that was Prince Boris, really.

'Nah, let's leave the future be.' The Doctor shrugged. It was exactly the tone of the lady next door about her cat's massacre of the dawn chorus. It's just a cat. They don't know any better. Sometimes the Doctor can be both patronising and chilling. He whirled around. 'Which is the point – Time is like a big messy house of cards that just keeps teetering higher and higher into infinity. So brilliant, so delicate, so much of it. And you don't want to go fiddling with any of the cards. Believe me.' He clapped his hands together and caviar went all up the walls. 'Broken hearts everywhere.' He spun round again. 'Dr Bloom really is amazing. He's curing people from a dreadful disease, but he's doing it about a hundred years early.

And that's not good.' He glanced at the ground and looked a bit sheepish. Eventually he continued, the words dragged out of him. In that moment his great, stretchy rubber face was so kind and so sad. 'Which brings me to you, Prince Boris. And I'm sorry, but here's the thing… I think you're one of the nicest Russian aristocrats I've ever met and not been forced into an arranged marriage with. You are kind and brilliant and make lovely coffee and probably ensure that every one of your serfs gets a goose at Christmas. That's good. And what's dreadful is that you've got this awful wasting disease… a disease that will shorten your life. Only it isn't doing that any more, is it?' Suddenly, without moving, the Doctor was staring out the window, no longer looking Boris in the eye. Like he couldn't bear to. Boris had gone very, very still, every word the clang of a dreadful bell. 'You are getting better. And I really don't think you should be. It's not just you, either…'

Rory took my hand. He knew what was coming.

'You see… this place is expensive. You've got to be rich to come here. Which, sad to say, in this time means that you're probably important. Maria's mother has a lovely house in Paris. A really lovely house in Paris. Practically a palace, isn't it, Maria?'

Maria nodded solemnly. She looked so scared. I held out my hand, and she came and perched on my lap.

It was just the four of us against him. Four lonely, scared humans staring at the dreadful alien. Who just wouldn't shut up.

'Even nasty old Mr Nevil is actually an MP. Hard to believe it of someone with such awful table manners, but there we are. I hate to say it, but if he lives ten more years, that's ten more years before people stand a chance of electing someone nice.' The Doctor stopped, his hands in his pockets, glaring out of the window down at the sea. 'Then there's silent Helena Elquitine – she's doing advanced logarithmic tables a decade before the man who dreams up the computer is even born. She's utterly amazing – imagine if she finished her work – Napoleon might have radar and remote-controlled missiles.' He glared at Boris and Maria sternly. 'Please forget I've even said the words *Napoleon* or *radar* immediately.'

Prince Boris tried to look nonchalantly bored, but I could tell he was deeply interested.

The Doctor carried on. 'Every single patient here is part of the house of cards that makes up history. If it was just the odd one or two then I could look the other way… but no. Every one of you.' He faltered, miserable. 'Every single one of you.'

The Doctor sank down on the end of the bed, not looking at us. A wind started up outside, rattling against the window, pulling cold air through the room. The Doctor's voice was so quiet I barely heard him over it. 'I hate my life sometimes,' he sighed.

Rory spoke. If I ever, ever forget why I love him, it's for moments like this. When we've been overcharged in a restaurant or the Doctor's sentenced a whole load of innocent people to death. No one else knows what to say, but Rory will just say something. He looked just as pained as the Doctor – not surprising since he's just had the Doctor's memories stamping around in his head. 'So it's got to be stopped – but what's causing it?'

'Oh, not Dr Bloom, poor silly booby.' The Doctor spread caviar on a cracker, the knife scraping away at it over and over and over again. I knew then he'd never eat it. He was just looking for something to do. 'It's those creatures in the sea. They're called The Familiar. You'll find them through Earth history – lonely travellers guided across a treacherous moor by the figure of a long-dead loved one, or the spirit of an old friend. That's kind of them. Living ghosts drifting from world to world, a well-meaning and barely sentient water-dwelling hive. They're… The worst thing is they're pretty much benevolent in themselves. But… oh, you know how it is, you land on a strange planet, meet a glamorous stranger who looks cool… they're easily led. And something… there's something here that is exerting an evil influence over The Familiar. They've formed a strong psychic link with something or someone nearby… and it's not good.'

'Fascinating,' muttered Prince Boris.

The Doctor crumbled his biscuit, watching the flakes land on the bedspread the wrong way up. Someone would have to clean that, I thought sadly.

'They probably don't even realise they're being used, bless 'em.' He groaned. 'It's all such a mess.' He threw his arms up in the air. 'Cards everywhere.' He flashed us a sad smile.

Boris started to protest. He'd suddenly put on the Aristocratic Air and it suited him very well indeed. He demanded an explanation, why, in all the many months he'd been here, he blustered, he thundered, he threatened, and then, eventually, he went very, very quiet.

'Kosov,' he said.

'Yes?' The Doctor sounded patient and kind. All the time in the world.

'If I tell you I had a difficult childhood, you'll just laugh. The fine son of a very rich family, while thousands and thousands of children toiled on my farms hacking turnips out of the frozen soil. But… mine is a cold country. I was never alone with my parents. Always in big, gloomy rooms with a distant fire and lots of people watching. My father was severe, always grave – and if there was a twinkle in his eye, I was never close enough to see it. My mother, oh, the hour a day I saw her, she seemed like a goddess from another world. But the rest of the time was the nursery and the schoolroom. The only person who ever seemed to care or like me was Kosov. He worked in the stables, and he laughed and he joked and he taught me to ride and he encouraged me and he seemed proud of me... and... well, he was like a proper father. He had his own family, but he always seemed pleased to see me. I liked that. I liked him. But oddly, you know, you move away, you send the odd present, but it's never easy to find out how your old stablemaster is doing. And then... then you fall ill, and you do nothing with your life. All those dreams, pointless. It all feels a waste... and then a countess discretely whispers at a party about this place. How marvellous it all is, especially with Kosov here again, looking after me.'

The Doctor nodded. 'You see?' he said, like he was scoring a point he wasn't happy about.

'I see,' murmured Boris, sadly. 'Could Kosov be working with these creatures somehow?'

'I don't know.' The Doctor's hands were jammed in his pockets, his gaze fixed on the beach. 'I'm not quite sure what's going on. But I'm open to suggestions.'

We argued about this. About what he was going to do.

It took us a while to realise that someone was missing.

Dr Bloom's Journal

Disaster!

I was standing on the beach with Kosov. Even my wife was frowning.

'The Doctor was not Familiar,' said Kosov sadly. 'The Doctor that The Sea created... lost...' He gestured out to the grey watery horizon. 'We need the Doctor.'

Perdita patted him on the arm comfortingly. 'Don't worry – we'll find him and Madame Pond. We'll find all of them.'

I made to protest, but Perdita stilled me with a glance. 'My dear, you worry about so much – leave this to us.'

She is always so kind to me.

We stood there for a minute, listening to the song of The Sea, watching the other patients dancing gently around each other. There was a light rain. There always was a light rain, and The Sea churned a dull grey, little flecks of white floating on top of it like snowy mountains or sleeping gulls.

Behind us, we heard a cough.

'Hello,' said a voice. 'Could I have a word?'

We turned. Standing there was poor Rory Williams. He waved, nervously.

What a funny little man, I thought. His face still looked soft and foolish, even if it was set with determination. Kosov grabbed hold of him, the fog pouring out of his mouth, but I stayed him. Perdita put on an interested smile, and Mr Williams continued.

'It's just… well, I thought I'd come and… talk to you. Before it gets… before it gets unpleasant.' Mr Williams looked as though he wanted to run away. I remember confessing to my father about stealing apples. He was trying desperately hard to be brave. 'I think the right thing to do, the fair thing to do, is for me to tell you about the Doctor.'

We looked at him. He was offering us just what we wanted. The Sea washed in, The Sea washed out. We waited, eagerly. Some of my charges say that I am not a patient man, but this is not true. A good doctor learns the art of waiting, of letting things play themselves out, of not interfering. Many is the time I have sat up with the dying. I know that they will find peace in the end. But in between sometimes they shout, laugh or cry. It is rare the dying wish to play cards.

Eventually, Mr Williams spoke. 'Right then,' he said, eyes darting around the beach. 'The Doctor. I understand him so well right now, because I've had bits of him bubbling around in my head. You see, the thing is, what you're trying to do, Dr Bloom, is so good. You are trying to cure a terrible disease – and you've got so much of it right. Fresh air, clean linen, sterile equipment, lots of rest. But whatever it is that's in The Sea… it's wrong, somehow. It's using you. And, at the moment, it's simply a difference of opinion between the Doctor and you. You both want the best. You've only tried to kill him a couple of times.'

I argued at that grossly unfair accusation. But Mr Williams pressed on, his voice getting firmer. 'I mean, don't worry about that. I've seen people do much worse to him and at the end of the day he'll take them out for pizza. He's very forgiving. The Doctor is brilliant.'

Perdita spoke, her voice carrying across the beach. 'So is my husband,' she said warmly. 'My husband is a wonderful man. Your Doctor wants to keep us in the Dark Ages. My husband is changing the world.'

'I think that's rather the problem.' Mr Williams stopped again. A bird flew overhead, calling out a warning.

'Go on,' said my wife, smiling.

'The thing is, when the Doctor decides something is wrong, he doesn't stop until he gets what he wants.' Mr Williams pulled a face at that, as though worried about something personal. 'You see… the Doctor always wins. And if he decides that he's got to stop you, then he will.' Mr Williams looked at us all, and smiled slightly.

'Is that it?' asked Perdita.

He shook his head. 'I just… You're doing such good work, and I don't want to see it all… wasted… just because he…' Mr Williams stopped and started tracing a pattern in the wet sand with his shoe. 'Well, he's not exactly subtle.'

'Are you threatening us, sir?' I rumbled.

He shook his head. 'Oh no. Really, no. I'm just saying… just for once… I'd like a simple life. You know. For the Doctor and the people he's up against to just sit down, have a chat, sort things out. It'd be a change. Cos I'm getting fed up of the alternative.'

'What's that?' asked Perdita sweetly.

Mr Williams pointed down to the sand. With his foot he'd written the word 'BOOM'.

'Anyway…' He shrugged, no longer nervous, just sad. 'I wanted to try. I can see it hasn't worked, but I tried. Just once.

And I'm sure he'll be happy to know that he was right. Because he always is. If it's all right with you, I'm going to go now – unless you want to knock me out and tie me up or something. Whatever.' And, looking tiny and miserable, Rory Williams turned and walked away.

I watched him go.

He got a few paces before he stopped. At first I thought he was going to turn around and say something else. Instead, he coughed. And coughed again, wrapping his arms around himself as though trying to hold himself in. He fought for breath, but the coughing wouldn't stop. Perdita looked at me, her eyes bright.

'Are you feeling all right, Mr Williams?' I asked, stepping up to him.

He stood there, staring at me, hand still covering his mouth. He lifted his hand away and stared at it.

'What's happening to me?' His voice was faint.

I put an arm around his shoulder. 'Mr Williams…' My tone was grave. 'You are extremely ill.'

He was still staring at his palm. It was covered in blood.

WHAT AMY REMEMBERED

'Rory's not my pet dog!' I yelled at the Doctor.

'Well, that would be better.' He was truly angry. 'Dogs I can live with.' He paused, suddenly hopeful. 'Quite sure you're not more of a cat person?'

'This isn't getting him back,' I said.

He pulled a face. 'Who said I wanted him back? I was just suggesting a few alternatives. Nice little ginger tom. Have to get it neutered, of course.' He smiled winningly. 'I'd let you name him.'

'We'll find Rory.' I was firm. 'And then neuter him.' I flopped down on the bed.

Prince Boris patted my arm sympathetically. 'Have you been married long, my dear?' I guessed he was making a 'women, eh?' face at the Doctor. I caught him at it, and he flushed slightly.

The Doctor pointed at the window. 'Out there, Amy Pond, is an alien intelligence that is about to shred human history. Now, who do you want popping off to have a word with it – a thousand-year-old Time Lord or a mostly qualified male nurse?'

'Don't say it like that,' I hissed.

'Well, what do you want me to say?' The Doctor was so angry he was almost hovering. 'Well done on marrying the only male nurse not to have a full set of Barbra Streisand records? Why did you pick him, anyway? Were there no flight attendants in your village?'

'Only Jeff.'

'Ah.'

I stood up. I stood up quite a lot. It takes a bit to stand eyeball-to-eyeball with the Doctor. It's not just that he's taller. It's that his eyes are like... it's like looking into something you shouldn't. When I was young there was a solar eclipse and we had to peer at it through cards or combs or some such in case you went blind – and everyone sneaked a peek directly at it, anyway. At this rolling, burning light that rubbed away at your eyes. The Doctor's gaze is like that. Only with slightly kissable eyebrows.

'I picked Rory, always Rory, because he is just like you,' I yelled at him. 'He is sweet and understanding and funny and he always tries to do the right thing. Plus you both run the same way.'

'We do not.'

'Do so.'

The Doctor and I both sank down onto a sofa opposite Prince Boris who was trying his best to look like he wasn't there, poor sock.

The Doctor puffed up like he was about to shout, then flexed a leg. When he spoke again, his voice was soft. 'You really think I'm like that? And you really think he's like that?'

I nodded. Thing is, it was complicated. You can't talk about these things with the Doctor because they always slide off the wrong way. He's odd about emotions sometimes. Like he's crossing them off in a Spotter's Guide. 'Ah, yes, that'll be

Anger, that'll be Fear, and I've a hunch that's Love. Tick tick tick.' I imagine him sitting around chatting to his friends (does he have friends?), saying, 'Humans, eh? Sometimes you can almost tell what they're thinking.' And yet at other times it's like he's spent a hundred years living out every emotion, one at a time.

Don't even get me started on the whole Doctor-Amy-Rory thing. It's kind of like… I dunno. Suppose you'd always fancied Ryan Reynolds. That's fine, yeah. You meet someone else, who is maybe not Ryan Reynolds, but perhaps he's got the same goofy smile. And you think, 'Yeah, that's it, I'm happy.' Then Ryan Reynolds himself roars up in a camper van and says 'Hey guys! Let's all go on a road trip. Bring the boyfriend! It'll be fun.' Only Ryan Reynolds doesn't save the universe. Well, not at weekends.

So I guess that's my life. Crammed in a camper van, sneaking the odd glance at Ryan, squeezing the hand of my lovely husband, staring very hard at the map and wondering where we're going.

Look, while I've been ranting along like this, well… not much has happened really. I mean, that's a lot of thinking going on, but it only takes a couple of seconds – all these thoughts are whizzing through my head at like a million, million miles an hour. So heaven knows what it's like in the Doctor's brain. I imagine it's like someone built a large hadron collider in a candyfloss factory.

It's clear we're not saying anything. We're just sat there, on a sofa. The Doctor and Amy Pond. Not currently saving the universe. Not currently shouting at each other, either. So there's progress.

Prince Boris got up. 'No, no, stay there,' he protested, with a theatrical cough. 'I am only a dying Prince, of course it's absolutely no trouble at all for me to make you some more fresh tea.'

That broke the mood.

We bustled around making the tea. All this time, Maria had been sat watching us, her eyes as wide as saucers. Big curious saucers. She tugged at the Doctor's sleeve. 'Is this all real?'

The Doctor crouched down. 'Does it feel real, Maria?'

She nodded solemnly.

The Doctor tapped her ever so gently on the nose. 'Then it is real. Remember that for ever.'

'But…' She looked at him, almost scandalised that a grown-up was saying this. 'It just…'

The Doctor, still somehow squatting, grinned. 'Maria, you've seen it all with your own eyes. Don't doubt it for an instant. When you grow up – remember that. If you see it, it is real.'

She nodded, very solemnly. Frankly, he was giving it 110 per cent, but it was only inches away from 'always let your conscience be your guide'. But I could tell that, from that moment on, the Doctor had a friend for life.

Maria carried on looking at him. 'I like Monsieur Rory very much. He was very kind to me. Please don't leave him on his own.'

The Doctor stared at her, blinked, and grabbed a cup of tea from Prince Boris. He dropped three cubes of sugar into it, drained it in a gulp and winced.

Then he glanced at me. Not the full Oncoming Truck brilliance, but a sly little look. The closest he'll ever give me to 'you win'. Very, very quietly the Doctor spoke.

'Amy Pond, Tiddles will have to wait. We're going to go and rescue your husband.'

THE STORY OF RORY

Hello. My name's Rory, and I'm dying.

I've not really said much so far. I've kept out of it. To be honest, I'd much rather let everyone else get on with it.

But it's complicated. I mean, Amy always knows exactly what to do. Even if she doesn't, she acts like she does. Running through a burning spaceship, laughing. Trust me, she's just the same down the supermarket.

Every now and then, I get left behind.

I love you, Amy Pond. I know that.

I really think you love me too. Sometimes. Well, I wonder if it's just that you really, really, really love me because you do, and sometimes if it's just that you slightly love me just because of the way that meeting the Doctor meddled with your childhood. If you see what I mean. See, now, that bit makes me cross. Cross because I don't like that thought as it works out badly whatever way you look at it. I'm cross that the Doctor messed up your head, but if he hadn't, perhaps we wouldn't be married. So maybe I should be grateful. The next thing I tell you is a lie, the last thing I told you was the truth. Bang.

Of course, now the Doctor's messed with my head too, and

I really don't know what to think any more.

The Doctor once told me off for dropping litter. We were on a lovely alien planet. Walking through a park of singing purple trees. And I dropped something. Now don't get all cross, not a tin can or anything. Just a banana skin.

It was like I'd dropped a grenade. The Doctor can't have heard it, but he stopped walking and turned around, glaring at me.

'What did you just do?'

'Nothing.'

'No, really, what? No one does nothing, not ever.'

I shrugged.

The Doctor took a step closer.

I felt my mouth go dry and wondered if this was how Daleks felt. Sudden urge for a wee.

His eyes drifted down, pointedly at the floor.

I followed his gaze.

Banana skin.

Amy came bounding up. Little bit like Tigger. If Tigger could totally rock a mini-skirt. 'Oh, come on, Doctor, it's just a banana skin.'

'Yes.' The Doctor spoke slowly. 'A. Banana. Skin.'

'Sorry,' I said. 'It's biodegradable, but fine. I'll, ah, pick it up.'

The Doctor's hand grasped my wrist. 'Repeat the B word.'

'What? Biodegradable?'

'Yes.'

I humoured him. 'Biodegradable.' Not like I fancied walking home.

The Doctor's next words came out like a hiss. It reminded me of that history teacher at school. Everyone has one – the one who just loves scoring points and leaving nasty notes in your homework in red pen. 'This is an alien planet. A totally unique ecosystem. A world that has, up until this precise moment, had no bananas on it. And you've dropped one casually onto it.'

'As I said, sorry, I'll pick it up…'

'You have infected this planet, Rory. Imagine what could happen next. That banana could decay, some stray seeds could germinate, and grow and lots of banana trees could sprout, all over the place. Who knows what could happen next? In five years' time this forest could be utterly dead. No more singing trees. Do you know what – these are the only singing trees for quite a number of star systems. So famous that, when many, many thousands of years from now, when two terrible warring armies meet in this solar system and find this world, what will they do? Will they fight over it? No, they land, and they just look at the trees and listen to them sing. About three hundred yards to the left and five thousand and three years from now, they declare peace. But no. That no longer happens. Not now. Instead they'll find a dead world, and their war will carry on for thousands more years until both civilisations, billions of people are dead. All because you have just dropped a banana skin.'

I was very, very quiet. Very quiet indeed.

'Pick it up, now,' said the Doctor.

I pocketed the banana skin.

'Thank you,' said the Doctor. He smiled. 'Of course, it won't happen. Bananas are good. I'm just saying.'

We walked on.

You see, that's the kind of grand gesture he loves. But every now and then I wonder, does he realise the mess he's made of Amy Pond? It's a brilliant mess, and it's a mess I absolutely love, but I wonder if he knows it's all his fault. And if he does know, does it keep him awake at nights too?

I'm just saying. It's all really complicated. I don't pretend to understand it.

So anyway, imagine how it feels. You're trying to do something brave. Instead, the bad people you're trying to reason with are suddenly, awfully, being really kind.

After I'd stopped coughing, Dr Bloom sat me down in his study. He shut the French windows, and his wife handed me a glass of something. 'No brandy, I'm afraid,' she said. 'It's quite a dry sherry.'

I sipped it. I didn't taste it. I tried to stop coughing. It wasn't easy.

'My poor boy,' said Dr Bloom. 'How long have you felt like this?'

He passed me a handkerchief of his own. It had 'J.B.' embroidered on it and some flowers. It's funny what you notice. There was a buzzing in my ears.

Strange. You work in a hospital, you see it all. The saintly old lady who had a fall and banged her head and woke up in a bed screaming and raging at everyone until she died, like she was suddenly letting go of ninety years of anger. The people getting thinner and yellower who still laughed at sitcoms. The worried looks that every patient had when they thought no one noticed. The mothers who came in every day to visit their sick children and tried ever so hard not to look bored, ever.

You see people dealing with bad news in a lot of different ways. Some people burst into tears there and then. Some made jokes about it and only went quiet when they thought they were alone. Some just went numb until the very end.

I guess that's me. The weak, silent type.

I mean, I was sat in a nice chair in front of a warm fire and

I was coughing up blood. And the coughing gradually ebbed away. Just a little. Then it came back.

I had tuberculosis. My lungs were being eaten from the inside out. Slowly but surely and utterly lethally. Which was weird. I mean, you do still get it in the twenty-first century. It does dreadful, dreadful things to people. But… there are pills and treatments and all sorts of wonders.

And suddenly I was over two hundred years away from all that. I was just sat in a chair, sipping sherry and fighting for every breath. It was all a bit confusing. There was also an odd feeling. Like the grimness of it all was pressing down on me. Like I was dying, right there, so far away from home, from Amy.

'How long do I have?'

Why did I even ask that?

Dr Bloom chuckled and patted my hand. Not in a patronising way. 'My dear fellow, you mustn't give up hope already. You are in the very best place for this. This is your very first attack, yes?'

He leaned over me, and pressed his ear to my chest. 'Hmmm. The left aureoles are rupturing. Don't worry about that as a phrase. It's all good. All good. So long as we know. Just breathe and breathe.'

'Can you stop the coughing?' I asked. It's actually really very horrible coughing up blood. True fact.

He shook his head sadly. 'It will pass. Just let it pass. Drink. Relax. You are in very capable hands, Mr Williams.'

I sank back into the chair. Suddenly I saw them all. Mrs Bloom looking so kind. Kosov stern. Dr Bloom eager.

'What will happen to me?'

Dr Bloom sat there. 'Don't worry. Just relax.' He patted my hand, and it felt good.

I was very ill. I was in a time without antibiotics. Without aspirin. I was so scared. I drank the sherry, feeling it burn the back of my throat.

'How… how have I got this?' I asked.

He shrugged. 'I am afraid you are… Well, this is a clinic. You are surrounded by the sick.'

I nodded at that. What a stupid thing to ask. Of course I'd become infected.

'Amy!' I cried. 'Please, find my wife. Find my wife and tell her.'

Dr Bloom nodded. All games were off. 'Of course. It's the least we can do. Where should dear Kosov look? I should hate to have him traipsing fruitlessly through the clinic.'

'Prince Boris's room.'

'Ah, yes. Of course.'

Kosov nodded, and left the room.

Dr Bloom leaned closer. 'Don't worry, Mr Williams. You are in good hands. Just lean back and relax. The fit will pass and then we can begin the treatment.'

I was so scared. I was so scared.

I had a sudden thought – the Doctor wouldn't let me die, would he? Not back here in history? It would be so easy for him to just nip into the TARDIS, grab a few pills and…

And then I realised. I could imagine the look on the Doctor's face when he found out. Because I had already seen it. Sad and angry.

Would he save me or leave me lying there?

Because I am just a banana skin on the ground.

A Letter from Mr Nevil

St Christophe
7th December 1783

Dear Octavius,

Is there anything so unaccountable as woman? You would think that anyone would be pleased that a fellow is feeling a bit better and no longer breathes like a broken bellows. But no! Not our precious Miss Olivia Elquitine. The dashed hussy actually gave me the Cut Absolute when I met her in the breakfast room earlier.

Her *froideur* is quite unaccountable! Simply because I am going down to that beach. It's a rough bit of cheddar that she's not allowed down there, but I have spoken to Mrs Bloom about it and apparently the treatment just isn't available to everyone. Which is a real shame – especially as Miss Elquitine's thin sister is allowed down there.

I cornered Olivia by the pastries and tried reasoning with her, but she wasn't having any of it.

'I am pleased at your good health, sir,' she said coldly, deftly unclasping herself from my hand.

'But blast it, Olivia,' I protested, flushing as I used her first name. 'I just want you to be happy for me!'

'You have nothing but my kindest regards, Mr Nevil.' She managed a chilly little bow. Why, if someone treated me like that in the House of Commons, I would knock the fellow down without a second thought!

Instead, I kept my head. 'It's a deuced shame that you're not allowed down there, my girl, but I can intercede with the Blooms. I am not without influence.'

'Indeed?' She arched an eyebrow. 'Does it not strike you as wrong that a cure is available only for those with influence?'

'Well, no,' I said without thinking. 'After all, there's rather too many people aren't there? Something like this, good for thinning out the common herd.'

I can't think why, but she just blinked at that, bade me a good day, and left me. As I said, women are unfathomable creatures!

The treatment itself is unaccountable. My memories are of a pleasant daydream and of Stoker, the dog I had when I was a child. Oh, there was never such a hound as faithful Stoker. Why, he smelt like a drain, but he was ever so good-natured. Funny how one suddenly remembers such things.

In other news, this place continues to be a veritable madhouse. Those three new visitors turn out to be crazy – the two men were pretending to be each other as some piece of foolery, or worse. I ask you Octavius – what kind of chap pretends to be a lady's husband? That sort of thing is all very well for poets, but not at a respectable resort. Of course, one of the men is now reported to be on his deathbed, which serves him right, if you ask me.

As ever, your faithful servant, etc.

Henry

Dr Bloom's Journal

Win them over with kindness! It works as well with enemies as it does with difficult patients.

The Doctor walked into the conservatory. Neutral ground. I bowed to him.

'It is a pleasure to meet you properly, my dear sir,' I said to him. So, I thought, looking him up and down, this is the creature that The Sea is so interested in, the brain so interesting it hid itself. There we were, scrabbling for Amy Pond or for poor blithering Mr Williams, and there he was all the time, neatly evading us.

Can what Kosov whispered to me have been true – that this was a man, not just from beyond this world but from beyond time itself? Personally, I thought he looked like a rather haughty student from my home in Geneva, right down to the studiously ramshackle attire. Yet, those eyes – those eyes were flashing with intelligence. He'd certainly done a lot to avoid the attempts of The Familiars from The Sea to read him – which merely made them want to read him all the more. They hungered for him so much I could feel them pushing down on my thoughts. With an effort, I cleared my head.

I noticed the Doctor just stood there, wary. Waiting for my move.

'It is all right, my dear sir, rest assured… I had Kosov call for you with only the best of intentions.' I tried on a warm smile. 'If I could wave a flag of truce, I would.'

'Go on,' he seemed arrogant, smug. Well, that would go in a minute. I nodded to Perdita, and the dear angel laid down two cups of steaming chocolate for us. The Doctor sat, scraping his iron chair across the tiling and made an elaborate fuss of looking around before settling himself, as wary as a caged animal.

'Well, I must say, this is all very civilised but it's not the same without a marshmallow.' The Doctor glared at the cup of chocolate that my Perdita had put in front of him. I ignored the rudeness.

'All the same, monsieur, it is excellent, I assure you. Perdita makes an unparalleled cup of chocolate.'

The Doctor sipped experimentally at the cup and then smiled. He nodded to Perdita. 'Wonderful, madame. My compliments. And not poisoned either.'

Perdita returned his nod with more politeness than he deserved.

I forced a chuckle. 'Come now, Doctor. Neutral territory, sir.'

The Doctor glared at me.

'Come, let's be reasonable,' I said, spreading my hands out.

The Doctor banged his hands on the table. The cup jumped. A little chocolate spilt over the edge. 'I am being reasonable. Where is Rory?'

'He is… indisposed.'

'What does that mean? You've kidnapped him?'

'Not at all… I regret to say…' It's hard doing this. Imparting bad news. Even to someone you can't actually stand. I have always hated causing pain. Physical or mental. Sometimes it is like striking a physical blow.

'Your friend. Mr Williams…' I continued.

'What have you done to him?'

'Nothing. Believe me, dear sir. But he is not well.'

'What?' The Doctor went pale.

'Indeed.' I put on my most candid expression. 'He is in an advanced state of consumption.'

The Doctor looked as though he was about to say something. He stopped. He stared at me. In some ways, I was pleased. He didn't say 'you're wrong', 'you're lying', 'there must be a mistake'. He just looked at me. And nodded.

'You haven't done this to him?'

'You have my word. I have taken the Hippocratic Oath. I am bound not to cause harm to others.'

'But how… how has he caught it?'

'How does anyone catch this dreadful illness? I have dedicated my life to eradicating it. You know this.'

'It's just…' The Doctor stood up and stared out to sea. He pointed out the one thing that had been nagging at me. He wanted to shut down my clinic. The clinic that had become the only way of curing his friend. 'It's highly convenient.'

'None of my doing.'

'And yet… And yet… If I was to tell you that there was a force manipulating events… driving us to this… Well, you'd see my point?'

'I'd see your point, yes.'

'So, if I were to tell you that, whatever you've been promised, you're not to trust it… would you believe me?'

I looked the Doctor over, carefully, before replying. What kind of man was he, I wondered?

'I have given my life over to progress, monsieur,' I told him. 'Surely you can see that sometimes Fate itself takes a hand? Look at the happy accidents that have led to great progress – in order for someone to invent a wheel, they must surely have seen a log roll down a hill. The secret of bread, the genius of a candle… perhaps animal fat dripped onto the fire and burned, or some flour went mouldy on a hot day… but imagine the hand that sits behind creation, nudging these events along… it is a remarkable hand, and sometimes, rarely, we can glimpse its movements.'

The Doctor shook his head, obstinate. 'Fate does not make my friends ill.'

'Perhaps, in this case, monsieur, it has. In order to make you see the bigger picture.'

'So… I have to let you cure him?' The Doctor stood up, the chair scraping along the tiles. 'Thank you for the chocolate. Much nicer than having a gun pointed at me. Can Amy see him?'

I spread out my hands. 'But of course.'

THE STORY OF RORY

I was on the beach. In a chair. The wind was blowing like a gale. Amy leaned over me. 'Hey, babes. I've pulled up your blanket.'

'Thanks,' I said, trying not to cough. 'It's really not so cold out here, once you get used to it.'

She nodded. 'Yeah.'

'You look very beautiful,' I told her. 'Windswept.'

She laughed. 'Thanks. It's the autumn look. Pale and interesting. How are you feeling?'

I coughed a little. 'Scared.' I managed a brave smile.

In the distance, I could hear something singing... a strangely tuneless noise that I vaguely remembered.

She hugged me. 'I'm scared too.'

'I'm a bit lost... There wasn't much call to know about tuberculosis in Leadworth.'

She smiled. 'Well, no.'

'It's kind of like knowing about Bubonic Plague. Or scurvy, you know.'

'Yeah.'

'I'm kind of glad to be a bit in ignorance. Medical people make the worst patients. We always know exactly what's going on. It's terrifying.'

'You're doing really well, though.' She squeezed my shoulder reassuringly.

'Kind of. I'm just sitting here.' I shrugged, but it was difficult.

'That's probably a good thing.'

'You think so, Amy?'

'I don't know. It's so odd. It feels like something dreadful is going to happen.' Amy stopped, and she shifted slightly, uncomfortable. 'It's just... Do you think the Doctor is right? Do you think this should all be stopped?'

I looked at Amy. I looked at the beach all around us. The wind tugging at the lonely tufts of grass. At a distance were some of the other patients, sleeping or nodding or murmuring quietly in their chairs. At the strange sea.

'I don't know. I'm just so scared, I can't think straight.' I stopped. 'I mean, I know I should tell you that the Doctor will save me. But I'm just not sure this time.'

'Do you trust him?'

'You do. That's all that matters.'

'OK. But what if... what if I told you I don't think he's right? What if I were to say that... that I don't think this clinic is so bad? That the Doctor wants to shut it down. To let everyone here die. I mean, that's not right, is it?' She tugged at my blanket, neatening it.

I laughed. 'We're supposed to save planets and people. That's why we travel through time.'

Amy repeated my words, nodding. 'Is it?'

'Good point. I mean, he's never actually said that. It just happens to us, doesn't it? We turn up somewhere and when we leave, things are normally better. Remember that cafe?'

'Which one?'

'The one where the guy couldn't make an omelette.'

'Oh yeah.' Amy smiled. It was a tight little smile. As though she was humouring me.

'And the Doctor said, "Claude, you can't make an omelette without breaking eggs," and taught him how to make a really good omelette, while telling us lots of stories about breakfasts with Napoleon and Churchill and Cleopatra. While we ate omelettes. So many omelettes.'

Amy nodded, grinning.

'Point is… we can't even go for a meal without him trying to make things better. But at the same time…'

'You can't do it without breaking eggs,' Amy finished for me.

'Yeah,' I said.

I noticed the fog drifting in across the beach, glowing gently.

'It's coming,' said Amy.

'Yeah.'

'Scared?'

'A bit.'

'Don't be. I'm here for you.'

Amy wrapped her arms around me, and I felt a little better. The fog spread itself around us both, a sickly green.

'Amy—'

'Shhh…'

Rory Williams. Sat in a deckchair. On a beach. About to be devoured by an alien fog. For my own good. With my wife there to help me through it.

One more thing.

One thing I'd forgotten.

Neither of us had mentioned that I was tied to this chair.

'You're not really Amy, are you?' I said.

'Shhh,' she whispered in my ear, and the fog flowed over us both, pushing the world a long way away.

Dr Bloom's Journal

7th December 1783

Impudence!

Kosov tells me that I am sent for by Prince Boris. Sent for! I am not his servant!

I thought for a moment about not going, but Perdita urged me to attend. 'It would look very bad if you did not go. He practically pays for the entire clinic, my dear.'

There was, as ever, truth in her words…

I traipsed over to Prince Boris's rooms. He was sitting there, a weak smile on his tired face.

'And how are you feeling, Your Highness?' I asked, my best professional manner shrugged on like a comfortable old jacket.

He waved this pleasantry away. 'Ach! Dear Dr Bloom, you know I feel amazing! Kosov and I,' he chuckled, 'have much to thank you for, really.' He closed his eyes for a moment, ever so tired. The wretched man is so lazy I wonder how he can even breathe. 'One feels almost invigorated,' he told me with a yawn.

'Indeed, sir,' I said. Truth to tell, I hadn't much time for this. Mr Williams was on the beach, telling The Sea all he knew, and the Doctor and Amy… soon, soon they'd agree to what I wanted. But I had to dance attendance on this yawning fool. 'So, how can I help you?' I tried to keep the impatience from my voice.

Prince Boris seemed asleep for a moment, then slyly popped open an eyelid.

'Actually, my dear Bloom, it is I who can be of help to you,' he said with a smirk. 'Finally, I am feeling like the man I should have been all these years. My head is clearer. My lungs are fresh. And I owe it all to you. So, my dear sir, I shall give you a gift.' He dropped his voice so low it scraped along the floor.

He reached into his desk drawer and pulled out a muslin-wrapped bundle. He unwrapped it with a flourish and dropped it onto his breakfast tray, where it landed with a loud, metallic thump.

I stared at it. In horror.

Prince Boris chuckled at my reaction. 'Oh come now, Bloom, surely you have seen one of these before…'

I shook my head.

'Ah, then you are in for a treat. This was made for me by a silversmith in St Petersburg.'

'You brought this into my establishment?' I was aghast. I mean, plainly, stupidly asking obvious questions. Clearly he had. It was there. On the tray, a gun nestled absurdly amongst the eggshells, cold toast and teaspoons.

Prince Boris didn't even bother replying. Instead he picked it up and turned it until it caught the light. 'It is a lovely gun, Bloom. And the time is coming when you will need it.'

'Never!' I cried automatically.

Boris nodded sagely. 'You love your wife, don't you?'

Outraged, I demanded he explain himself.

He cleared his throat. 'I cannot pretend that I can see the

future… but Bloom, I know things. I know terrible things. Allow me to make a prediction. Very soon, someone will try and kill your wife. I pray they won't succeed. But if they try…' He wrapped my hands around the gun. It felt cold, ever so cold. 'I want you to be protected.'

His voice hung in the air. I stared at him, at the gun, and then at him again. He didn't blink.

He nodded, gravely serious. 'Please, Bloom. Take this gun.'

He was so stern. Almost as if he was issuing an order.

I pocketed the gun and then didn't know what to do. There really isn't a social precedent for a man telling you that someone will try and kill your wife and then handing you a firearm. There just isn't. So instead I found myself talking banalities to him about his treatment. I even fluffed up one of his pillows and then, as quickly as I could, I left his room.

As I walked down the stairs, the gun weighed heavily in my jacket, like it was trying to pull itself free from my pocket with every step.

I made it back to my study and sat down, heavily.

When I was quite sure I was alone, I pulled the weapon from my pocket and held it, turning it around and around in the candlelight.

'*Someone will try and kill your wife…*'

WHAT AMY REMEMBERED

I sat down, numb.

The Doctor repeated what he'd just said, but there was just a buzzing noise in my head.

'I'm cold,' I said, rubbing my shoulders.

That didn't seem to be the reply the Doctor was waiting for, but stuff that.

'Did you hear what I said about Rory?' his voice was slow and patient.

I nodded. 'Yeah. But I'm cold. Really cold.'

'I see.' The Doctor looked around the conservatory. It was freezing and there was what looked like sleet coming down. Big, loud drops of rain fell on the filthy glass roof. It's funny where mould gets – pretty much everywhere, really. Even on a glass roof.

I'm sure the conservatory was cheery enough in the summer – it wasn't really a greenhouse, but more of a fancy shed nailed onto the side of the building. But, you know, stuffed full of plants. All of them looking like they needed a blanket and a cup of cocoa.

The Doctor stood over me, all concern and fumbly fingers.

'It's all right, Doctor, I'm not in shock. I just want to know what we're going to do about it.' I took a deep breath. 'So, Rory's dying?'

'Well…'

'Is he?'

'He… Amy… I'm so sorry…'

'Yeah. I just wanted to know. Can I see him? Where is he?'

'I don't know.'

'What? Of all the times to lose him. Can't we get him space medicine from the TARDIS?'

The Doctor pulled a face. 'Um.'

'What?'

'I've lost the TARDIS as well.'

I was outraged. Considering my husband was dying and we were stranded in the past, the Doctor seemed fairly calm about things. 'Someone's nicked it!'

'Not so much, no.' The Doctor looked awkward. 'There's a mechanism… thingy. If the TARDIS senses a threat it removes itself from the scene. First sign of danger, it goes and hides behind the curtains.'

'Whose genius idea was that?'

The Doctor swallowed, embarrassed. He claims to be the last of the most advanced race in the universe. Sometimes I'm just not convinced.

'Well, look, it sounds like a good idea on paper. But when your life is one long "Kill the Doctor!", having a spaceship that jumps a couple of hundred yards to the left when you really need it is a bit of a pain. So it's mostly switched off. But when we crashed we overloaded the buffers on the warp transfer coil, which would have switched it on. Good old Hostile Action Displacement System. I've missed you like a hole in the head.' The Doctor's arms were starting to windmill with awkwardness.

'And where is the TARDIS now?' I demanded. The only thing that could save Rory was missing, and the Doctor just seemed mildly embarrassed.

'Um…' The Doctor looked like he'd happily answer any other question. 'No sign of it yet. I think it's shifted in time as well.'

'So it's of no help to us?'

'Not really – but it can't have gone far.' He held up – he actually held up – two thumbs, as though this was good news. 'The translation circuits are still working, which means you haven't had to learn French in a hurry. And I haven't had to learn English. That's something.'

'Wait… what?'

You know those toddlers you see being dragged around supermarkets constantly asking 'Why are oranges orange?' and 'Can I have a biscuit?' while their parents try and get on with shopping… Sometimes, just sometimes, I wonder if that's how the Doctor sees me. This was one of those moments. There am I yelling 'Save Rory! We're trapped in time!' And the Doctor's trying to read the expiry date on a packet of digestives.

'That's really not important right now.' He seemed to have read my mood. 'Thing is, either the TARDIS is about to turn up, or The Familiar have got it.'

'So anyway, big picture – no drugs from the TARDIS. The best hope for Rory is Dr Bloom.'

The Doctor looked a little more nervous. 'You see, sometimes, you know when someone tells you something that you're not actually, at surface value, going to necessarily like, but, if you just think about it… well…'

I felt cold and scared. 'He's not on the beach, is he?'

The Doctor nodded glumly. 'I think he might be.'

I shoved him in the shoulder. 'Are you mad? Let's go and rescue him!' Sometimes he needs a bit of a push, bless him.

'No.'

'What?' My stomach lurched. Not my Rory. The Doctor just didn't get it. Rory is too important.

He tried to explain. 'If he is out there, then the very last place we can go is near him. We're too late. They're reading him.'

'We've been on the beach loads.'

'But I was shielding you every time.' The Doctor had adopted his 'being reasonable' tone. It was infuriating. 'Amy, if they've started reading him, I can't stop it.'

'What are they going to do to him? How can he help them?' I swallowed, desperately. 'He's just Rory.'

The Doctor's hand stroked my chin. 'There is no *Just* about Rory, Pond. Not any more. He's full of space and time and the universe. He's knows about you, about me, about the TARDIS. Think of everything he can tell them.'

I did.

I broke away from the Doctor, running towards the door. I had to get down to the beach. I had to rescue my husband. Now.

The Doctor grabbed my hair. For a moment I was pedalling like some cartoon character. Then I was howling in pain.

'Sorry,' he said.

I started hitting him, shouting and screaming at him. And he just carried on holding me. A tiny bit of my brain registered that down the corridor Miss Elquitine was playing her violin, that a storm was coming, that the carpet really needed sweeping. But mostly I was just furious with the Doctor.

He leaned forward, touching his forehead to mine. 'Think about it,' he said, his voice ever so gentle. 'Think about everything you know. Everything I know... and then about what Rory knows.'

I gulped. Really, awfully, terribly, I had a sudden attack of hiccups. I was staring at the Doctor, murderously angry with him. And hiccupping.

'He doesn't know as much as you, or me!' I shouted in between gasps. 'That's it. I'm going down there. I'm offering myself to them instead. If you're too much of a coward.'

The Doctor winced at that last word.

I hiccupped again.

'Amy Pond,' he said. 'Try holding your breath.'

'I will not hold my breath! This is important! Rory is having his mind vacuumed and we're just standing here—'

'Hiccupping.'

'Yes.'

We stood, glaring at each other. I hiccupped again.

'Seriously,' said the Doctor, patiently. 'I know it's not the best time, but really, try holding your breath.'

I stood there. Hiccupping and scowling at him.

'Rory knows plenty... but not enough. He's like a tasty little snack. He'll get them all excited about me, which should, just should, stop them doing anything bad to him.'

'Hiccup.' I stared at him.

'He'll be fine, seriously.' The Doctor smiled. 'They'll cure him. They'll do everything they can to keep him alive. Because as soon as they've read him, they'll realise that the very last thing they want to do is to upset me.'

I nodded. And hiccupped again. He stroked my face. His hands felt cold.

'I am so sorry, Amy Pond.' The Doctor's smile faded. 'It's just wrong. I know it is. But it's the best thing I can think of. Really it is.' He grasped my shoulders. 'Sometimes, that's all I can manage. I am so sorry about Rory. And I am sorry about this…'

I have no idea where he got the ice cube from. But it slid suddenly down the back of my neck. I gasped and stopped hiccupping.

'There we are.' The Doctor tickled me under the chin. 'One problem solved. If only everything else was that easy.'

DR BLOOM'S JOURNAL

All I am venturing to say is… surely a life of peace isn't too much to ask, is it?

Nothing extraordinary – it's just that everything was finally going to plan. The creature in The Sea assured me that once it had read the mind of Mr Williams it would have everything it needed. I had followed all of its instructions. We had a bargain. I had given them my patients and it had cured them.

There have been times when I have wondered if I have really been doing the right thing. But luckily I have Perdita, ever present Perdita, to come and squeeze my hand and tell me it's for the greater good.

It hasn't always been easy. Sometimes someone has come to the clinic, someone in desperate need of a cure, and I have had them wheeled down to the beach just once, only to receive a message – 'I'm afraid they have nothing we want.' And I have had to watch them die.

It wasn't like that to begin with. At the start, The Sea wanted everyone. Everyone I could give it. Then it became picky.

My brother is a terribly fussy eater – boneless fish, only certain cuts of meat, and carrots and potatoes. Curiously,

I've observed that picky fellows never have a problem with puddings. Odd that. The beach became just the same – refusing simple people with just enough money for the cure. It only wanted powerful people, or army people, or government people. It couldn't get enough of them.

I would ask, I would ask several times, 'Surely, you have enough now? Can't you begin curing the others, please?'

The answer would come back: 'Soon, soon, but first, we must understand your world. We must have more.'

So I would bring more.

For the record, I must just point out that this goes against my every principle as a medical man. People must be cured, irrespective of who they are. But it's all very well standing on a beach trying to deliver a lecture on medical ethics. There's a story of a king who tried to prove his power by ordering the tide not to come in. He stood on the shore shouting until he drowned. It was a bit like that. The Sea made it plainly apparent that it was not to be ordered. It was quite nice about it, but very firm.

It was incredibly interested in Prince Boris. That's why it assigned Kosov to follow him around personally. 'This one is… this one is of much interest to us. He is lazy and sleepy and yet… his family is so cruel. Underneath all that indolence is a genius. A military genius. He will do much. Much for us. We cannot wait until we have made him better. Both in his body and in his mind.'

I obeyed them. What choice did I have?

Finally, just finally, I thought, I could sit down. Just sit down in my chair for a few minutes and look at the fire and think about everything. We were learning everything we needed to from poor Mr Williams. We had Prince Boris firmly under Kosov's control. We were at last winning. We even had the

Doctor running scared – he knew that if he didn't help us, Mr Williams wouldn't be cured.

Surely everything was finally going to plan, wasn't it? The matter of the gun and the warning from Prince Boris worried me, but I dismissed them. Sometimes it was nice to sit in front of the fire and admire your winning hand.

'*Someone will try and kill your wife…*'

The thought kept returning to me, even as I sat in front of the fire. I could not enjoy even a moment's peace.

WHAT AMY REMEMBERED

We went to the lounge, which was almost empty. The string quartet was now just the thinner Miss Elquitine, playing the violin in between fits of coughing. Scattered around the lounge were a few patients, pale as ghosts, clutching their armchairs like they were using them to grip on to life. In the corner an old lady with no teeth was slurping a cup of broth as if it was her last meal.

'Not everyone gets cured, then?' I asked the Doctor.

He shrugged sadly. 'Only the important people. Another reason I don't like what's going on here.'

'You're sure Rory is perfectly safe?'

'Oh yes.' The Doctor waved an arm around. 'He can't tell them anything useful. Don't worry. Trust me. When they realise there's nothing there, they'll let him go. It'll be fine. Especially after I've done the next bit.' He rubbed his hands together and then coughed loudly.

Miss Elquitine stopped playing her violin, and a hush settled over the room.

'Ladies, Gentlemen, Boys and Girls,' began the Doctor. 'If I might have a word…'

It was kind of like when Hercule Poirot calls everyone into

a room to say who did it, although at first everyone in the lounge looked totally uninterested. But the Doctor spoke on. He explained a lot of things – about who he was, about who they were, about why they were here. About all sorts, really.

'The most important thing to know is that you all have a dreadful, dreadful disease – and you came here looking for a cure. Some of you are still waiting for that cure. The bad news is that the cure won't work.'

At around about this point, some of the nurses sidled into the room, their faces sharp and interested. The Doctor spoke on. 'There is a time for everyone. And I'm afraid to say, your time has come. You were all born too early. Dr Bloom is a brilliant man, but his cure won't work. It can't be allowed to.'

Helena Elquitine stood, with a little difficulty, her thin frame shaking, and pointed her violin bow at the Doctor. For a second, she looked about to speak, and then sat back down.

A tall, pale-skinned man started shouting at the Doctor. 'What are you saying? That we're dying?' He laughed, a wet and deep laugh. 'We've known that for years… but some of us… some of us have started to hope… that maybe one day we could be cured.'

The Doctor winced. 'I'm here to take that hope away, sorry.'

That went down very badly. Jedward badly.

'Tough crowd,' I whispered to the Doctor.

He glared at me, furious. 'Not now, Amy.'

I winced. But he'd already turned back to them, walking slowly around the room, like there was all the time in the world, talking to each one, so kind and patient. Trying to reason with them, to explain. To tell them all that they were going to have to die. He did it very nicely, I'll say that for him. Like he was coaxing and encouraging and cajoling. But he was still spreading really very bad news.

As the Doctor talked, I noticed other patients slip in to listen to him. Mr Nevil came in, followed stiffly by the plump Elquitine sister. The Doctor started talking to a tiny, frail old man who was shaking his head sadly. I pointed out that we really should go, that we were running out of time.

'So are these people, Amy,' said the Doctor, straightening the old man's blanket. He patted the man on the knee.

Olivia Elquitine stood at his side, shaking with fury. 'What if you're lying?' she hissed, jabbing him with a plump finger.

The Doctor looked at her, so dreadfully still. You know how it is when it's about to rain and there's just a fraction of a second before the heavens open when the world pauses and braces itself? That's how still the Doctor was.

'Olivia, you know I'm not lying. You know. I am sorry.' He patted her on the shoulder.

Mr Nevil was next, the great brute of a man looking scared. He was huge, old and large, but now he just looked like a scared little boy. Olivia grasped his hand protectively.

At that moment, Dr Bloom made his grand entrance with his wife at his side. They looked magnificently cross. Dr Bloom was in full sail, but Mrs Bloom got there first.

'My dear Doctor!' she shouted. 'What do you think you're doing?' She flashed a smile around the entire room. 'Oh dear, whatever next! You really mustn't be up and about, must you now?' She took an arm, and tugged it firmly. 'The poor man's had quite a nasty bump. We'd better get you back to your room before you have Another One.' She underlined the last two words very neatly. 'And you, dear Madame Pond.' Her voice was as sugary as a honey-coated knife. 'Madame Pond. Here you are, up and around with that dreadful concussion of yours. Why, I do despair. If we're not careful we'll find you both dead in your beds tomorrow.'

That surprised me. A clear, actual threat from Mrs Bloom. Sugar-coated, but still. I raised an eyebrow.

She acknowledged the challenge with a tiny, tight little nod, as stiff as the ringlets in her hair. The nod, the smile – it all said, 'Oh yes, I know your game, and I am telling you right now that it stops.'

Olivia Elquitine stood up again. 'But Madame Bloom! Dr Bloom! He's been saying such dreadful things.'

Now it was Dr Bloom's turn, all soothing warmth. 'I am sure he has, my dear. This poor man is ever so ill!' He chuckled, like he was reading a Christmas cracker. 'Why, he even thinks he's a doctor!' More laughter. Which the Doctor joined in with. Startlingly.

He slapped Dr Bloom on the back. 'Absolutely. Hilarious. Naturally, I came in here to tell all your patients that they were going to die. Great joke. Lovely.'

The tiny old man looked up, eyes red and rheumy, and blinked. 'Are we still getting rice pudding?' he asked for no apparent reason. I was with him.

'Yes,' snapped the Doctor, angrily and coldly. 'There'll be rice pudding for you, buns for everyone and plenty of orange juice for the Silurians, too.'

Mrs Bloom tugged at his arm again, and found herself holding the Doctor's jacket. He'd slipped free of it.

He strode into the centre of the room. 'Dr Bloom, you are a brilliant, brilliant man, but you know that what you're trying to do is wrong – it's a short-cut, and it's a short-cut that isn't going to work. I'm going to give you a tip – fresh air, rest, lots of hygiene. That's all on the right lines. Stick with that. But stop, I absolutely beg you, stop trying to use that thing on the beach to cure these people. It's not going to work. It can't work.'

Dr Bloom smiled a slow 'got you' smile. 'If the cure is so wrong,' he said, 'why have you let me use it on your friend Mr Williams?'

'Ah.' The Doctor's manner fell. He was met by a storm of muttering protest from the patients.

Mrs Bloom was at his side in an instant, wrapping his jacket around his shoulders. 'See, Doctor, you've got yourself all in a dreadful tizzy. We really should just pop you back in bed. Come away now and stop making such a dreadful scene…'

The Doctor's reply, when it came, was very quiet; as soft as an old towel. 'I am letting you cure Rory because he shouldn't be here. He definitely shouldn't be sick. And because he's too important to Amy for me to let anything happen to him.'

'Interesting,' said Mrs Bloom, her words all gooey with caring. 'Can't you see what a muddle you're in? Tch! Tch! What a pickle! Perhaps it'll all seem clearer when you've had A Little Rest.' Clearly that was a signal – the attendants moved closer, gathering in around the Doctor. I wondered if they'd invented the padded cell yet.

'Oh, very good.' The Doctor frowned. 'You did it deliberately, didn't you? You infected Rory so that… so that…' He slumped, letting two attendants grab hold of him. I felt someone else grab my arm. So that was it then, rebellion over. Well, we've had better.

Dr Bloom started, frowning at the Doctor. 'I didn't!' he protested, his voice troubled. 'Please, I really must assure you.'

Eyeball-to-eyeball the Doctor replied, 'No, you didn't, did you? So if you didn't, who did?'

A crackling silence settled between the two of them.

Dr Bloom faltered. 'I don't… I mean… I don't know…'

The Doctor nodded. 'Something else is going on here, Dr Bloom. You think you're at the centre of the web – you're really a long way off. You're just a fly. So who is the spider?'

Dr Bloom's wife squeezed his shoulder. 'My husband is a very important man.'

'Yeah, yeah, yeah,' the Doctor looked bored. 'But... someone else is running things, aren't they?'

Perdita stood very still.

So did the other patients in the room.

It was electrifyingly odd.

'Oh,' said the Doctor. 'That's curious. It's been listening.'

'What?'

The Doctor waved around the room. 'Look at them... something has got into all their minds. Something very vicious and nasty.'

The patients stood there. Silently. Awkwardly. Staring at us.

'Er, Dr Bloom,' whispered the Doctor. 'I really, really think you should listen to me when I say this... Something is very badly wrong with your patients.'

'How so?' Dr Bloom looked baffled.

The patients all stepped forward. Shuffling closer. As one, they raised their hands. BANG! The French windows burst open and the storm started to pour in. The candles blew out... but the room stayed lit – a strange green glow was seeping up from the floor.

The Doctor looked at the Blooms and then at the patients.

'Right,' he said. 'Interesting. Fifty-seven varieties of interesting. Dr Bloom, you woke up something very alien but mostly benevolent on that beach. You saw a way to use it to cure people. Only something's taken control of that creature, and instead of using it to take bad things out of people... to cure them... only now, it's putting things back into them.'

'Really?' asked Dr Bloom.

One of the Elquitine sisters twisted slowly towards him, fog pouring from her mouth and clothes. The same thing was happening across the room – skirts and jackets billowing and leaking out a thick, green mist. It stank.

It was a terrible sight, so bad that it shook Mr Nevil from his trance. 'Olivia!' he roared. 'What's happening to her?' he demanded. 'Is this your doing, sir?'

'No,' the Doctor sounded alarmed. 'There is a strong psychic link between the thing on the beach and the patients. Someone has been using it to affect the patients and the creature…'

Inside the mist, lightning crackled – it was like the storm was in the room.

'That is very bad.' The Doctor shook his head, warding us back. 'That psychic link needs severing… It's not going to be pretty.'

Mr Nevil stood there, his hands shaking. 'I have a gun, sir, I have a gun!' he yelled, pulling one out.

'Well, please don't shoot it at the weather,' snapped the Doctor.

'Nonsense!' roared Nevil. 'I don't care about that. I'm going to take down a couple of these leaky blighters. Soon square them up sharpish.' He took aim. The Doctor reached out to push away his hand, but instead the storm acted – a bolt of lightning lashed out of the mist, striking the gun and wrapping Nevil in St Elmo's Fire. He stood there, jerking and yelling like an angry puppet toad and then stopped.

The light around him faded – the room was dark now, dark apart from the crackling green fog that was pouring out of Mr Nevil's mouth.

'It's the storm,' I said. 'How are they doing that?'

'Tell you in a minute.' The Doctor grabbed my hand. 'I need you all to get out of here…'

The lounge was changed – the shutters were banging wide open in the rain, and the fog was pouring in through the windows – that same fog from the beach, curling up around everyone's feet and lighting the room a pale green glow.

Something pulled at my brain. I couldn't move. I looked at the Doctor, desperately, but there was something... something in my throat.

The Doctor seemed to realise. 'Please, hurry. It's me they're after...' He turned and shouted to the storm. 'Yeah, go on, lovely juicy brain. Come and get it!'

I could move my feet a little. 'What are you doing?' I demanded.

'Hopefully giving you all a bit of space. Run!' The Doctor stood there alone, confronted by the steadily advancing patients. Fancy dress zombies shuffling closer and closer towards him.

'Right,' I said. 'Come on.'

We made it to the door before the Doctor started to cry out. Whatever he was doing, it hurt him.

DR BLOOM'S JOURNAL

How we made it out of the room, I do not know. But there we were, in the corridor, nestled behind an aspidistra. Of the Doctor and Amy Pond there was no sign. From the lounge a rumble like thunder came. I could hear Perdita sobbing.

'What is happening?' I wailed, but for once, my marvellous wife had no answer.

'It's terrible, terrible,' she cried, clinging to me, smelling like rose petals. 'It's like something is pressing into my brain.' She kissed me. 'Oh, Johann, I'm so scared.'

Someone will try to kill your wife. I banished the thought, hurriedly. I gestured back to the lounge, my lounge, lit up like burning phosphor. 'What is going on? The patients, oh the patients…'

Perdita grabbed her head, shaking her ringlets free until they hung loose around her face. I'd never seen her hair like that. It looked… magnificent.

'Something has gone terribly wrong,' she whispered. 'I can feel it. Somehow… my head… The Sea… it is not happy. Someone has woken up and is taking hold…'

I held her close to me. What were we going to do?

WHAT AMY REMEMBERED

There was uproar in the lounge as we ran out. Absolute uproar. Thunderbolt and lightning, very, very frightening, etc. I've never liked storms or thunder but there was something worse about this. It seemed like the storm was in the room.

The Doctor caught up with me, hands pressed to his head. 'Well,' he groaned. 'That hurt.'

As we ran, he rattled on. 'Something is controlling that entity in the sea. Something very bad. It needs to be stopped. Right now we're in ALL SORTS of trouble. Say something encouraging, Amy.'

'I can't,' I said, struggling to keep up with him. 'But what's it using to make the storm?'

The Doctor stopped running. He looked at me. His face was really very pale indeed.

'Amy,' he said. 'You remember I told you that Rory was in no danger whatsoever and we weren't to worry about him?'

I hate him when he says stuff like this. It's almost like he's the anti-Santa. It's that dreadful, immediately sick in the stomach, utterly sad and miserable feeling. The utter, certain, kickingly dreadful knowledge that Things Are Not Going To Get Better.

The problem is that I know exactly what to do in this situation. You see, there's a drill:

1. I'll say, 'Right, then, let's go and rescue him.'
2. The Doctor will say, 'Ah yes, but…'
3. And then he'll list the fourteen things we have to do before we rescue Rory
4. And why they're all more important than rescuing Rory
5. The list normally includes wounded puppies
6. An exploding bus full of grannies
7. You know what I mean
8. So we'll go and do those instead
9. Cos they're all so important
10. And Rory has to come last.

I can already see the Doctor opening his mouth to explain.

'Oh, skip the lecture,' I growled and, before he had a chance, I ran off down to the beach. I was going to rescue Rory.

A Letter from Maria

St Christophe

7th December 1783

Dear Mother,

I got scared. For a while I was on my own in the clinic. And it was all quiet. I went back to my room and wrote letters and read a book. I kept out of trouble.

I looked down at the beach, but I could not see anything – just a lot of mist.

Eventually I left a letter for you in the post tray.

I heard footsteps behind me.

It was the Elquitine sisters. Standing there. Blocking me off. There was something NOT RIGHT about them. They were not smiling, just standing there, blankly.

I talked to them, but they did not answer.

Their heads swung from side to side, like the puppies when they're looking for something to hunt. Yes, that's it. The sisters were hunting.

Mother, I was frightened.

But I did not want to go outside. And I did not want to go towards them. I had to, but I did not want to.

I edged closer and closer, pressed up against the wall.

Their heads swung towards me, following my every footstep. They smiled, a cruel empty smile.

I edged past them and away. I did not look back. I knew they were watching me.

But THEY DIDN'T WANT ME. So that meant that I could run and run and run and I would be fine.

Wherever I went, there were other patients. In the corridors. Searching. Steadily searching. Moving ever so slowly forward. Like hungry ghosts.

I decided to rush upstairs to my room.

One step. Two steps. I crept up the stairs, feeling the wood creak beneath my feet. I tried to keep calm, to be brave. No worse than sleeping through a thunderstorm. No worse.

I reached the first landing and turned, and my legs turned to liquid.

Standing at the top of the stairs was another patient, the sad Austrian who couldn't play chess, his mouth set in a toothless leer. Ever so quiet. Waiting.

I threw open the door to the cupboard under the stairs and hid in there, quivering.

Suddenly.

Horribly.

I realised I was not alone in there. I could hear breathing.

Then a terrible green glow lit up the cupboard under the stairs. I was about to scream, and then something stifled me. Oh it was HORRID!

Mother, they were the worst moments, truly. But don't worry – see, I am writing this letter to you, so I must be fine. The Doctor made it all right in the end.

Then a voice said, 'Shhhh.'

It was the Doctor. He was looking at me. The green glow was the light from his sonic screwdriver. He looked awkward.

'Hello,' he whispered.

'Hello, monsieur,' I whispered back.

'Sorry about that,' he said. 'I was hiding.'

'Me too.'

'I know.'

'Are there, by any chance, an awful lot of patients roaming the corridors behaving most creepily?' he asked.

'Yes.' I nodded solemnly.

'Oh well,' he said. 'All my fault. Something has got into them. They're trying to find me. I gave them a tiny little bit of my brain. Not much. A few memories, a colour I never really cared for. Just enough to get away. The thing in the sea... it is taking hold of them. Something else has linked to it. Something powerful and dreadful that has only now realised what it can do. The psychic link must be broken. I think I know who it is, but... No.'

'What are you going to do about it, monsieur?' I asked him.

He groaned. 'Why does it always have to be me?'

'Mr Rory is ill. You're the next best thing,' I said simply.

'Thank you,' he muttered. He didn't sound very pleased at that at all.

'I can go and get Mr Rory, if you want. He'll know what to do. But he probably shouldn't be disturbed.'

'No...' the Doctor agreed with me. 'He's ill and...' He sighed. 'The thing is... I could stop all of this so easily. I just... It's not the right thing to do.'

'Then what is, monsieur?' I asked.

The Doctor smiled at that. 'Well, Maria, I should like you to be very brave and to go and find Prince Boris. See if he can reason with Kosov... he's got a very strong connection to that thing in the sea. Maybe it's Kosov who is controlling it. Don't tell them where I am, but see if... see if Prince Boris can influence Kosov somehow. Things are very bad… but I think you can help me.'

He squeezed my hand.

'Don't worry, monsieur,' I assured him. 'I'll go.'

The Doctor smiled. 'Thank you,' he said. 'You are very brave.'

'What will you do?'

'I'm going to reason with Dr Bloom. Before it's too late.'

Your ever loving

Maria

THE STORY OF RORY

So there I am, talking to a fake alien version of my wife. And the truth is, it's not so bad, actually.

Now, no, don't look at me like that. There are things that you can write down that sometimes you can't say to someone. No matter how much you love them. Because you love them.

There was a time when Amy really liked going clubbing. I've never been one of life's dancers – I can jig around a beer bottle and that's pretty much it. But not Amy – she's hands in the air, woo, for hours and hours and hours. She even knows all the moves to 'Single Ladies'. And, of course, there aren't really clubs in Leadworth, so someone has to be the designated driver. That'll be me. Rory Williams. Standing by the coats in the corner, swaying gently around an orange juice while Amy's out there in the dry ice, laughing and dancing. She's having a good time, so I stand there, pretending very hard, with a desperate grin on my face. Because I love her. And if I let on that I am bored out of my mind, then maybe she'll leave me. I don't want that to happen. So there's me, and the coats, and the orange juice, hoping the wheels will still be on the Subaru when we finally leave New York. By which I mean New York the nightclub, so good they named it just the once.

It's the same when we're travelling around the universe, actually. Don't get me wrong – it's amazing, it genuinely is. But there are times – just times, when you think, 'I would quite like a say, if that's OK.' Nothing grand. Just a choice of planet or something. Rather than finding yourself in a nightclub on Space Florida, holding the coats and yet another lukewarm orange juice, watching the Doctor and Amy dance.

They've gone now. I'm abandoned. They're not coming for me. They've probably forgotten about me already. Got in the TARDIS (*what's that?* whispered a voice)… Yeah, got in the TARDIS and gone. Gone off through time and space (*time and space?*). Leaving me behind on a beach, talking with a version of my wife. And she is actually listening to me.

'Right then,' I said. 'I don't suppose you'd mind telling me what the plan is, would you?'

'Silly,' she said, tapping me lightly on the nose. 'The Sea and I are going to make you all better.' She tipped her head on one side and smiled. 'You do want that, don't you?'

'Yes,' I said. Because I am scared. So scared of dying here that I am letting this happen. 'But why – why are you doing this to me?'

She shrugged. 'It's what we do, lover boy. We are very good at it.'

'But…?' I prod.

'Clever thing,' she laughed. 'Well, we can only do it by reading your mind fully. We haven't been able to do that yet. It takes time. Even this version of me is just skimmed from your surface memories.'

'My brain?' I said. 'But why would you want to read my brain? I'm nothing special.'

Amy paused, and ruffled my hair. 'Of course you're not, durr.' She blew a raspberry. It was oddly chilling. 'The mind

170

we really want to read is the Doctor's. But we haven't been able to get into it, yet. So you'll just have to do.'

Story of my life, I think, as the mist wraps itself around me.

A Letter from Maria

St Christophe
7th December 1783

Dear Mother,

It is no longer like a fairy tale. I am scared and lonely and I wish that you would come for me. It's been a terrible day. But the Doctor sent me to see Prince Boris. I hoped that maybe he would say something nice, or give me a candy, or play a card game with me. Instead, he looked ever so sad. He was out of bed for once, standing at the window, not saying anything, so I went and I tugged at his sleeve.

He smiled down at me, but it was ever such a tiny smile. He lifted me up and hugged me, his great big beard scratching at my cheek until I laughed.

'It tickles! It TICKLES!' I protested.

He put me down and patted me gently on the head. 'You're going to have to be ever so brave, little Maria,' he said. 'We all are.'

'Does that mean that you will play cards with me?' I asked.

He gave a weary nod, and we went to the card table. He shuffled expertly, talking of the many games of chance that he had played and won. He promised to teach me the fine game

172

of poker. It sounded most interesting. I knew there were other things I must do, but I do like games.

There was a sharp rap at the door, and Kosov walked in. When I saw him I shrieked and dived under the bed. Kosov was after me at once, his giant arms stretching under the bed frame. 'Come here, come here you little wretch!' he bellowed, but I was far too quick for him, wriggling out and darting into a corner. Kosov clambered to his feet and lumbered over to me. I cried out.

'Oh, what is the meaning of this?' Prince Boris managed to sound bored at the same time as commanding.

'Oh monsieur!' I protested. 'He will kill me, truly he will KILL me!'

Kosov made a rumbling noise, an ugly smile on his face. 'The child does not understand. She needs treatment.'

'I do not!' I protested hotly. 'I am fine. Oh, Prince Boris, you know you must not trust your servant. You know he is working with Dr Bloom. You know it!'

Prince Boris sadly tied and retied his fine red dressing gown, leaned back against the wall and looked between us. 'What a mess,' he chuckled, but there didn't seem to be anything funny. 'You two are both so noisy!' He yawned. 'I am such a lazy man, and yet no one will leave me alone.' He glared at me, like an ogre in a play. 'Maria, if I wished for children I would have got married, but all the women I met were artful shrews who liked diamonds and dresses a shade too much.'

'What about Madame Amy?'

'Ha!' laughed Prince Boris, 'We'll see how she treats Monsieur Rory.' He turned to Kosov. 'And you, my man... you...'

'Keep back, Prince!' I urged. 'Keep back!'

Prince Boris smiled a tiny little smile, and advanced to

Kosov. The giant of a man stood there. Prince Boris walked around him, tiny little steps, still tugging at the cord of his dressing gown. 'Are you really here to kill me, Kosov?'

There was a terrible silence for a second. Then Kosov bowed. 'I am here to serve you, Your Highness. Your health is my top concern.'

'Indeed.' Boris fiddled with the sash on his dressing gown cord. 'Indeed. And how old are you?'

Kosov blinked. 'I am 35, sir.'

'I see. And if you are 35, how old were you when you taught me to ride as a little boy?'

Kosov faltered. 'It was so long ago, Your Highness.'

Prince Boris nodded. 'We are now the same age, Kosov. Yet, you taught me to ride when I was 4 years old. Explain that.'

Kosov just stood there. Eventually he said, 'But Your Highness, there must be some mistake…'

Prince Boris shook his head, all the light gone from his face. 'There is not. And never, ever contradict me. How old are you?'

Kosov took a trembling step towards the Prince. 'Please, sir, don't do this' he cried, reaching out a trembling hand, imploringly. The giant begging from the prince.

But Prince Boris had folded his arms. Suddenly, for the first time, I realised what he was like when he was really a prince, rather than a bored man in pyjamas. His face was no longer light, or gay or charming. It was grim and sharp like the executioner's axe.

'So, Kosov, tell me – are the Doctor and Madame Pond in danger?'

Kosov stood there, sad but insolent.

'What is Dr Bloom planning?'

Again, Kosov shook his head.

'Very well. What are you?'

Kosov did not move.

'Ah.' Prince Boris let the word hang in the air. 'You know what, Kosov, my dear chap? I rather fancy going home. I miss it all. Even in winter. There's nothing quite like coming in from a cold horse ride through the forests to a roaring fire and a boiling dish of tea. I rather think I shall send for my things and go home. I am cured.'

Kosov made a noise, like something broke inside him. He breathed out, raggedly, like an injured dog.

'But I shall go home alone, I rather fancy. Perhaps via Paris. Yes, a few days there. And quite a lot of late nights. Just the ticket after all Dr Bloom's thin soup. When I get back to the estate, perhaps I shall send for you.'

Kosov shook his head, the sweat running from his brow – if it was sweat?

'Or maybe,' continued Prince Boris, 'I shall simply saddle up my horse and go out, riding, riding, riding, every day through the frost. How marvellous would that be!'

Finally, Kosov spoke, his voice twisted. 'Your Highness, I beg of you…'

Prince Boris shrugged and laughed, 'Oh Kosov, dear Kosov, you're not real. Go away and haunt some other fellow. You're nothing but a Golem.'

Kosov took another step forward. 'Please… you must believe… please, you have to… It's for your own good…'

Now it was Prince Boris who shook his head, his eyes cold and blue. 'No, Kosov. No. If you were the real Kosov, then I wouldn't even doubt why you were doing this. He loved me like a son, and I adored him. I used to dream about working in the stables with him – oh, what stupid childish dreams. I'm sure it was a hard enough life. But Kosov was a great man.

You, sir, are not Kosov. So I have to ask the questions I ask every man who approaches me with a deal that's too good to be true: why are you here, and what is in it for you?'

Kosov's mouth hung open. A little, wet clicking noise came out of it.

'No answer?' said Prince Boris, almost sadly. 'I just wish… Ah well. You may go.' He turned his back on Kosov and stared out of the window. 'I have no more need of you.'

I crouched in my corner, watching.

For a while, Kosov just stood there. I thought he might cry, or walk away, or do any one of a number of things. But he just staggered. A false step. His balance shifting, almost as though… no, half of him sank to the ground. And his face! His face was like ice, running and melting and falling apart. Even his clothes dripped like hot wax.

I watched for as long as I could. But as the strange thing shattered, it made a dreadful gurgling noise. Like it was crying.

That wasn't the worst thing. The worst thing was that Prince Boris laughed.

That was when I ran away.

Your ever loving

Maria

Dr Bloom's Journal

Perdita sank against the wall. She looked dreadful.

'It's Kosov,' she croaked. 'Something has gone terribly wrong.'

'What?' I asked her.

She slid down, her head falling forward, her features hidden beneath that spilling tangle of hair. She moaned. 'It's too late… Go to him, Johann, please…'

I rushed up to Prince Boris's rooms, and found the Prince dressing himself. He was tying a cravat, perfectly, and didn't glance round from the mirror.

'Ah, Dr Bloom,' he purred, even managing something sarcastic in the click of his heels.

I stared at the thing on the floor. It looked… well, like a foggy lump of glowing clay, only matted with a lot of wet hair. Sometimes the clinic cat will vomit up a half-digested rat on the study carpet. It was just like that, only bigger. There was a dreadful smell coming from it. It was still moving, slightly, damply. It was horribly familiar.

'Was that Kosov?' I gasped.

Prince Boris winked at me. 'Poor Dr Bloom, you've gone

quite green. I thought you medical men had better stomachs.'

'What have you done with him?'

'I've killed him.' Prince Boris actually rolled his eyes. He flopped back on the bed. 'He'd cured me, so I had no more need of him. I simply wished him away.' He groaned theatrically. 'Oh to be able to do that with all the peasants back home.' He jumped up and rubbed his hands. 'Oh, I feel marvellous. I'm quite grateful to you, really I am. And so terribly, terribly sorry about the mess on your carpet.'

I tried not to look… What was this man?

He clasped his hands behind his back. 'Ah, now for the creature on the beach. What a marvellous thing it is! I cannot wait to meet it,' he announced. 'Many years ago my father sent me on a… diplomatic mission. It was slow, painful work. I applied myself rigorously to it for two whole days and then the third I stayed in bed.' He affected a yawn. 'I can sense that whatever that creature is… it is a marvel but it is used to being dealt with gently. You are a kind and patient man.' Boris shrugged, and tugged away at his loathsome beard. 'I am not.'

He let it hang there in the air. It was a threat. A definite threat.

He smiled suddenly, and tapped me on the chin, the kind of gesture you'd make to a pet. 'I owe it all to you, dear Johann.'

I flinched at the familiarity.

'I am a changed man! A changed man! I feel marvellous! For the first time in my life I have the energy to be exactly who I have always wanted to be.' He clapped me insolently on the shoulder. 'Now then, I think I should see whatever it is you're keeping on the beach.' There was a nasty glint in his eye. 'I think it's about time I showed it who really is boss.'

With that he sailed from the room.

As he left, he called over his shoulder: 'Don't forget my gift to you, Dr Bloom. It's very important.'

THE STORY OF RORY

Funny how you forget things. Such as whether or not the thing that looks exactly like your wife is actually your wife or not.

'Amy,' I said to her, completely forgetting that this wasn't Amy at all. 'I don't feel too well.'

The thing that looked just like her made a shushing motion and laid her fingertip on my lip. 'Don't you worry about a thing, my lovely Rory boy,' she whispered to me. 'We're nearly over and done with. You're just about cured. I'll even kiss it better.' And she smiled, a lovely smile that lit the entire beach a brilliant green.

Despite the gathering storm and the rain, a warm glow spread through me, like a cup of hot chocolate on a crazy cold day. I gave an experimental cough. No rattle. Nothing bad. Just a cough. And my head was clearing of fog. I felt amazing.

I turned around to the other patients, sat dozing next to me on the beach. 'Do you hear that?' I cried, 'I'm cured! I'm cured!'

A couple of them nodded, but they didn't really stir.

Amy tutted. 'Poor dears, it's taking a lot more to cure them. You know how it is.'

'Er… Why is that?'

'Well, I suppose there's no harm in telling you, now you're

all better.' Amy smirked. 'You… Well, you only had it a little. A tiny weeny little bit. Just enough…'

The lovely warm glow went. 'Just enough to make me trust you.'

Amy nodded. 'Sorry, hon.'

'But that's… Dr Bloom wouldn't…'

Amy stroked my hair, 'He had no idea.'

'So whose idea was it?'

And that's when a rather fussy, amazingly dressed figure glided out of the mist. It was Prince Boris, no longer in pyjamas but in a full *Prisoner of Zenda* military outfit. He strode towards me and bowed, clicking his heels. 'It was my idea,' he said, his voice warm and fruity. 'I suggested to Kosov that he give it to you.'

He turned sharply to Amy. 'Have you learned everything you need from him?'

She nodded, dully. There was something odd about the way she looked at him, fearful. 'We have learned a lot. He has been beyond this world. He has travelled through time.'

Prince Boris laughed. 'How utterly wonderful!' He looked at me with something like sneering respect. 'How novel! The Doctor mentioned something in small talk, but I am fascinated to know exactly how?'

'Not telling,' I said.

'In a blue box called TARDIS,' said Amy dully. 'He has no idea how it works. The only person who knows is the Doctor.'

'Ohhhhh,' said Boris, laughing again. 'How interesting. How very interesting. What about the girl?'

Amy shrugged. 'She is very important to this man. He worries she loves the Doctor.'

'Oi!' I cried. 'It's more complicated than that.'

Amy turned back to me and winked. 'No it isn't, babes.'

Prince Boris smirked. 'So you are jealous of your wife?'

I tried very, very hard to be brave. 'Well, who isn't?'

'Interesting,' sighed Prince Boris.

He grabbed hold of the thing that looked like Amy and kissed her, long and slow, watching me all the time. I hated him.

'Fun! Of course, if your wife cared for you at all, she would be here. But where is she?' He looked up and down the beach, like a pantomime villain, and then shrugged. 'Oh dear, my friend Rory, I don't think you're very important at all. Your companions have abandoned you…'

Tell me about it, I thought, miserable.

'They have abandoned you to me.' He grasped hold of the fake Amy, and twirled her around, laughing as they danced. 'I tell you, Mr Williams, these creatures have made me amazing! And they do respond ever so well to a strong mind. I'm just off to have a word with them. Tell them who is boss. Goodness me – what a waste I've made of my life. I'm making up for lost time!'

'What?' I narrowed my eyes at him. 'I thought you were nice!'

Prince Boris tutted and clucked his tongue at me, like an old lady in a sweet shop. 'No, not nice. Merely incredibly polite. Anyway, if you will excuse me…'

He made to go away, but Amy stopped him, resting a hand fondly on his shoulder.

'Yes.' He was irritated. 'What is it?'

'Now we have cured Mr Williams, can I release him and return to The Sea?'

Prince Boris shook his head. 'No, drain him dry.'

And with that he walked off into the mist.

Dr Bloom's Journal

7th December 1783

A fine, dreadful pickle, made all the easier by just how wonderful Perdita is to me. She squeezed my hand by the aspidistra. 'It will all be all right, my darling,' she said.

Sometimes her good mood infuriates me. I gestured to the corridor. 'How can it be? Prince Boris has taken over! He's ruined everything. The man's mad. I thought I just had to deal with the Doctor, but now this! I mean, look at it – my patients! The clinic is a shambles!'

Perdita looked at me. 'I know, my dear.'

'But what are we going to do?'

She considered this. 'I know someone who can help. But you won't like it at all, I'm afraid.'

Which is how we ended up outside the door of my own study, knocking on it. Infernal, infuriating cheek! But Perdita nodded, encouragingly, giving me the strength to carry on. I knocked and I waited. It was like waiting to see Herr Gustaffson back at the medical academy in Switzerland. I felt suddenly like a young man again, full of ideas and nerves and…

A Letter from Maria

St Christophe
7th December 1783

Oh Mother!

I'm so scared – this place is so dreadful! I simply can't stay here any longer. It's just utterly, utterly terrifying. First there's the storm and the mist – they're both filling up the corridors. Then there's the other patients. They're all behaving really oddly.

Finally there's Prince Boris, who is suddenly being REALLY NASTY.

He's like… Oh, you remember how Aunt Claudette was always ever so nice, and ever so lovely until Uncle Jean died and left her very rich and then she became impossible and cruel and had all of his dogs put down? It's like that, like he's suddenly got the chance to show off just how nasty he can be. I really don't like it. He's jolly unpleasant.

I ran back to the Doctor, who was still in the cupboard under the stairs, cradling his head.

'Monsieur Doctor,' I said to him. 'How are you? I have something to tell you!'

He shook his head sadly, 'Not now, Maria.'

I stopped.

He paused. 'Sorry, sorry, sorry. That was rude, wasn't it? I don't mean to be. It's just so much is happening and I've got everything wrong and I've lost Amy and my head hurts and I am pleased to see that you're not affected. That's one less thing to worry about. Actually, is it? If you don't mind, I'll just think about that…'

I burst into tears. It normally helps with grown-ups.

'Right,' he said. 'Sorry again. It's all a bit much, isn't it? Let's go and hide somewhere else. Somewhere with toast would be nice.'

We ended up in Dr Bloom's study, sitting in front of the fire.

'Thinky thinky think,' shouted the Doctor. He'd found a jar of biscuits and we were sharing them. They were ginger, and I didn't much like them, but I didn't want to say that to the Doctor as he looked ever so preoccupied and cross. I was bursting to tell him about Kosov, but the Doctor held up a hand. 'Now then, now then. Maria, I suppose the building isn't on fire, is it?'

I shook my head, solemnly.

'Ah well. That's one thing not to worry about. OK, then. Right.' He bit off half of a biscuit, chewed it a bit and then spat it out. 'How many of these have I eaten?'

'Four, monsieur.'

'Oh dear. I hate ginger biscuits. Eurch.' He screwed his face up. 'So, then, this is the problem. Dr Bloom's accidentally built a giant battle computer on the beach and I think someone has realised this, but who? Who? – No, don't interrupt, that's a biggie. Then there's all those people who have been cured who really shouldn't be. Then there's all of the knowledge that Dr Bloom has. Then there's Amy in danger. Or Rory who's in just as much trouble. Then there's the fact that the one machine that could stop all this is missing. It's a lot of problems, and I don't know where to start, and the taste of ginger really lingers, doesn't it?'

See, Mother, this is what the Doctor is like. I worry about having him to stay. I'm sure he'd write things on the tablecloth. And probably upset a few of the servants. But I do like him. Can we invite him, perhaps?

'Have I left anything out?' he asked me.

I shrugged. 'I'm a bit confused.'

'Me too,' he admitted. 'So what bit should we do something about first?'

I thought about this, swinging my legs a bit under the chair. 'Your friends, monsieur,' I said solemnly. 'They are important to you.'

'Well then, maybe. But what about Europe?'

I shrugged.

He took the last biscuit, chewed it, grimaced, and finally swallowed. 'Fine, then.'

There was a knock at the door.

'WHAT NOW?' snapped the Doctor.

I jabbed him with my elbow. 'I'm fairly sure that's rude,' I admonished him.

'Whatever,' he tutted. 'Sorry! Come in!'

The door opened, and Dr Bloom walked in with his wife.

'If I could perhaps have a word?' he asked.

DR BLOOM'S JOURNAL

7th December 1783

'Come in!' The Doctor sounded impatient and actually cross at being disturbed.

'I do hope I'm not intruding,' I said, managing, I hoped, not to sound sarcastic.

The Doctor actually waved an arm around airily. 'Oh, not at all, not at all.' He handed me a tin. 'Biscuit?' he said.

The tin, I noticed, was empty. Perdita had made me those biscuits.

'Um,' he said, snatching the tin back. 'They're all gone. Don't worry, though, they were rubbish.' He pulled a face.

How dare he, how dare he.

Perdita placed a soothing hand on my shoulder.

'It's not going very well, is it, Dr Bloom – I did warn you.' The Doctor waved a finger at me like a patronising teacher.

I held my breath. Perdita stepped in. 'My husband is as alarmed by this turn of events as you are. Which is why we came to see you.'

'And you found me very quickly. Very quickly.' The Doctor glared at dear Perdita. 'I did wonder. Oh yes. Where are the rest of the patients?'

I shrugged. 'Roaming the grounds, perhaps. Or down on the beach. In this weather. It's not ideal. And Prince Boris—'

'Never mind,' snapped the Doctor. 'There's something you should know, Dr Bloom. There is a way of weakening the creature's psychic connection over the clinic, but I just don't want to use it. It's more important that I find out who is behind all this.'

I tried to tell him again, but that was, of course, when the French windows opened. And there was Prince Boris, striding in. It was quite an entrance. He was smiling and even swaggering a little.

'Doctor, you cannot be allowed to stop Dr Bloom's work. I forbid it.' He stopped, as though swallowing something. 'We can't have you standing in the way of progress, dear sir.'

The Doctor boggled at Boris. 'Prince Boris… are you… feeling all right?'

Boris paused for a second, his confidence fading. 'I… I don't know.' He pressed a hand to his temple. 'Something is pressing down on my head. My mind… Oh, Doctor.' He stretched out his hands, pleading. 'It hurts. Please… can you stop it? I'm not myself! I can't control my thoughts!' He staggered back against the wall.

'It's the psychic link,' said the Doctor grimly. 'I've got to stop whoever is controlling it.'

Boris looked up, his teeth gritted. 'I know. Please… stop it!'

The Doctor turned to me. His face looked so sad. I felt Perdita grip my hand.

'Dr Bloom…' he began, and then stopped.

'Do it!' urged Prince Boris. 'For pity's sake.' He gasped and stared at me. 'Damn you, Bloom, what about your wife?'

'Not Perdita!' I said. 'Not my dear wife. She wouldn't harm a hair on anyone's head. She is my rock.'

And then the Doctor did something dreadful.

I cannot believe what happened.

'Dr Bloom,' he began. 'I'm sorry, but how long have you known your wife?'

What a stupid question. I told him he was being an idiot.

'No, but really…?' The Doctor stared at me. 'Think about it. When did you first meet?'

I stared back at him.

Perdita squeezed my hand. 'Tell him, my dear.'

I stood there. Rooted to the spot. Feeling sick. I looked at Perdita. At her grip on my hand. At her smile.

'I… Does it matter?'

'Yes,' said the Doctor. 'It matters very much. I have to try and weaken the psychic grip of The Sea. I have to. And I have to do something. Tell me, Dr Bloom. When did you first meet your wife?'

I licked my lips and frowned. 'I can't remember.' I turned to Perdita. 'When did I meet you, dearest?'

She looked back at me and smiled. 'Whenever you say I met you, dearest.'

I staggered. My knees went. My stomach heaved. And yet I just carried on gripping her hand.

'No, Perdita, my love, when did we meet?'

She carried on looking at me, as calm as a lake.

Oh please, oh please, oh please, no.

'Whenever you say, dear,' she repeated. 'You always know what's best.'

I tried to look away from her, but I couldn't. I wanted to look the Doctor in the face and scream at him. But I kept looking at Perdita, at my rock, my guide, my best friend. 'Doctor,' I said.

'I know.' His voice was a whisper. 'Don't say it.'

'But…' I stroked Perdita's face, so warm and tender. 'My

Perdita… my dearest Perdita…'

'Dr Bloom, I am sorry.' It sounded almost like the Doctor was crying. I couldn't see. I didn't want to see. 'Your wife is a Familiar. She was never real. The Sea gave her to you. She's been guiding you, making you do what it wants all along. I am so sorry.'

Your wife is a Familiar.

Your wife is not real.

The Sea gave her to you.

I had a sudden memory. Of standing on the beach and suddenly feeling a hand in my hair. Moving ever so gently down and stroking my shoulder. A gentle warm laugh on a cold day. And there she was. Standing there. My wife.

Perdita tilted her head to one side. 'Dearest, what is he saying?'

'He's saying… he's saying… he's saying that you're not real.'

Perdita dismissed it with a laugh. 'But what does the Doctor know? He's half the man you are. You always know what's right. You always do.'

'No,' I said. 'Just this once… the Doctor is right.'

I squeezed her hand. And I shut my eyes. I'd seen what had happened to Kosov. I knew what was coming.

'I love you,' I said.

'I love you,' Perdita said back to me. And for the first time, the only time, I noticed how flat her voice was.

And then it started. A dreadful wet noise, like ice melting and falling from a roof.

When I opened my eyes, she had gone.

THE STORY OF RORY

'I feel dreadful,' I said.

Things to bear in mind – as I've said, I'm a really bad dancer. But there I was, dancing. On a beach. With Amy. In the rain. Without a butler holding an umbrella over us. All around, the rest of the patients were dancing. It was slow. Ever so slow.

They had come down from the chateau, all of them, walking in a slow shuffle, the mist rolling around them, pouring out of their sleeves. Maria had told me she called them the Dead, and they looked like the Dead now – strange, lifeless things dancing.

Some of them were crying. Mr Nevil waltzed past, holding grimly on to Olivia Elquitine, while a dog bounded around at their feet. 'My darling, I'm so tired,' he sobbed to her. 'So tired.' She clung to him, holding him up – who would have thought that it was her who had more strength?

'I know, my dear,' said Olivia, gently. 'But it's the dog, it won't let us stop.'

'I am so sorry,' sighed Mr Nevil. 'That's Stoker. Old fellow made me so happy. But not now... I don't need him, now that I've got you.' He squeezed her hand tighter and they danced on.

I looked at Amy, at the thing that was somehow Amy, as it dragged me on and on. 'Why are you doing this?'

She smiled at me, just a little. 'You're needed for fuel. All the patients are. For sustenance. For the storm.'

'Righto,' I said. I could feel my legs starting to buckle. 'Surely we can't do this for much longer?'

Amy tugged me further and further on. 'Until you drop,' she said.

A LETTER FROM MARIA

St Christophe

7th December 1783

Dear Mother,

I don't like the Doctor any more. He made Madame Bloom
go away.

I feel bad now for never liking her. I really do. But I can't
unwish all the bad things I've thought about her now. Or can
I, Mother, because I'd really like to?

I saw Dr Bloom's face then. How much he loved her. How
he couldn't bear to look at that thing on the carpet, that
bubbling thing that still had her hair.

I was very angry with the Doctor. I was furious with Prince
Boris for making him do it. But I was so cross with the Doctor.
I screamed at him.

He just nodded, ever so sad.

'I am sorry,' he said to the room. 'I am really, really sorry.
But… Dr Bloom… Johann… it had to be done.'

He had the air of someone who was hoping that what he'd
said was just true.

'The creature in the sea, it was feeding off of you. I had to
break that link. Now it's just a creature. All by itself.'

I wanted to tell him that he was wrong. But he wasn't listening. He was just staring at Dr Bloom.

'Open your eyes,' said the Doctor, gently, pleadingly. 'Please. Look at me and tell me you know that.'

There was silence in the air. I realised the Doctor wanted Dr Bloom to tell him that everything was all right. That he'd wished his wife away and that… that he forgave him. I wondered then… what kind of man was he? What did he think people were really like?

Dr Bloom shook his head. 'Has she gone?' he asked, his eyes screwed shut.

The Doctor grabbed a blanket from the back of a chair, and threw it over the thing on the carpet. I tried not to hear the wet noise it made. 'More… more or less,' he said. The Doctor rested a hand on Dr Bloom's shoulder. 'Johann, please… I had to. The psychic link. It's broken now.'

Which is when Prince Boris cleared his throat. 'Actually, no. You see, Doctor, I think you'll find it's just cleared the way for my link to the creature.'

'What?' The Doctor turned, gawping at him.

Prince Boris nodded. 'I took over from Dr Bloom some time ago, but he and his wife were resisting my influence. Now he isn't linked to it any more. I have you to thank for that.'

The Doctor just stood there.

I tugged his sleeve. 'Monsieur,' I said. 'I've been trying to tell you!'

'Ah,' the Doctor nodded. 'Always listen to children. Sorry, Maria. I'm sorry I didn't have time for you. So… Boris. Are you evil?'

'Not at all, my dear sir,' chuckled Boris.

'You just chuckled,' groaned the Doctor. 'Chuckling's a dead giveaway in my books. Along with putting your hands on your hips and snogging another man's wife.' He stuck his hands in his pockets. 'So…' he said. 'Let me get this right. I've just made a dreadful, terrible mistake, haven't I?'

Prince Boris laughed. 'Absolutely. Don't worry about it. We all make mistakes.'

The Doctor turned to Dr Bloom and sighed. 'I am so sorry.' He shook his head. 'Boris. What a shame. I liked you.'

Boris marched over, and patted the Doctor on the hair. 'And I liked you too, Doctor. But this… this is all such a splendid opportunity. You really must agree. It's brilliant.'

'Is it?' said the Doctor.

'Oh not this, this little clinic full of sad little people. But no, it's the thing down on the beach. It's really ever so marvellous. It's like a library – it's absorbed the minds of everyone here. It really is the most intelligent thing in the world. And I'm linked to it. To think I've wasted so much of my life. But luckily, when they created dear Kosov to cure me, I became linked to it. I could see into it. I could guide it. I could reach an arrangement with it.'

'What?' said the Doctor. 'You're what's been guiding The Familiar all along?'

'Well, not exactly all along. But… I've had a helping hand. I've shaped a few decisions. And now it's ready. It really is. It knows everything – who to trust in government, who is strong, who is feeble-minded, which are the really great armies, the natural leaders, and the weaknesses of every single country in Europe. Down there on the beach is a giant brain ready for war. And it's going to tell me everything I need to do in order to become the most powerful man in the world.'

'Oh,' said the Doctor.

The door opened. And the two Elquitine sisters shuffled in, their eyes blank.

'Aha! My army!' laughed Boris, 'Now then. It's time for you to go to The Sea, Doctor. The creature would very much like to meet you at last.'

THE STORY OF RORY

I am so weak.

The hospital once organised a Fun Run. There is, trust me, no such thing. I remember a miserable day running round and round Leadworth in the rain. Amy said she'd turn up and cheer me on, but she'd overslept. So her dad met me at the finishing line with a Tupperware box full of corned beef sandwiches and a mug of tea.

'Two hours of running, eh?' he said, sipping from his little plastic cup. 'How much did you make?'

'It's not the amount you raise, it's the taking part,' I explained, sensing I was on weak ground already. That's the thing about Amy's dad.

'Well, I'm sure that's a lot of consolation to the kids waiting for that new incubator.'

'Twelve pounds and thirteen pence,' I muttered miserably.

We sat there for a moment, chewing on sandwiches. There was a lot of chutney. Amy's dad likes chutney.

'I see,' he said, and handed me a twenty pound note. 'Come on, let's go and see if Princess Amy has woken up yet.'

*

I looked at fake Amy. Her perpetual smile and her frozen gaze. 'Please,' I said, shuffling. 'Please can we stop?'

'No,' she said. 'We've got to carry on dancing. We've got to. Not much longer now. Come on, babes.' And she dragged me round. I trod on her toes. I'd been doing that quite a lot, to be truthful. At first by accident, and then a bit maliciously. She never complained. She wasn't Amy. The real Amy had long ago abandoned me… Dancing to death…

She dragged me on, round and round that beach. Some of the other patients had already given up. Mr Nevil lay there, rain spattering over him, his dog tugging at his collar, trying to get him up again.

The storm crashed around us.

A hand tapped Amy on the shoulder.

'Hi,' said a voice. 'Can I cut in?'

It was Amy. Real Amy. Standing there. She hadn't forgotten me! She'd come to rescue me! She looked murderous.

Fake Amy smiled back at her, empty as ever.

'Well,' said Real Amy. 'Aren't you going to tell Rory he's a rubbish dancer? I know I would.'

'I love him,' said Fake Amy.

Real Amy rolled her eyes. 'Which of us do you prefer, husband dearest?' Her face narrowed dangerously. 'Think very carefully about your answer.'

'Well…' I began. 'She is very nice to me.'

'Rory Williams,' Real Amy thundered. 'You don't like nice.'

'It's a change.'

'I love you,' cooed Fake Amy. 'You dance so much better than the Doctor.'

'Silly.' Real Amy nudged her in the ribs. 'Hippos dance better than the Doctor.' She turned back to me. 'Rory, listen.

Very quickly. You have to say it out loud. I know you're thinking it… but you have to say it.'

'What?'

Amy tapped her duplicate again. 'Say it. Go on. About her.'

'That she's not real?'

'Perfect.' Amy laughed. 'Say it again, like you mean it.'

'Don't listen to her, my love!' Fake Amy looked at me, startled, then fell down, vanishing into the mist.

'Result!' Amy giggled, hugging me.

I held on to her. She smelt as wonderful as ever. I'd missed her so much.

'I am so tired,' I said, and fell asleep.

Dr Bloom's Journal

Fool! Fool! Fool!

This journal is the story of my life's work. Although now that my life is over, it seems strange that my work will continue.

It seems stupid to admit that I had no idea that so much of my life was a lie. Who was Perdita? Was she ever real? I have a vague memory – a memory of once talking to a charming woman as we shared a table by Lake Geneva, of sharing a sticky gateau. Was my wife based on that? Half a memory of a charming afternoon? Did The Sea give me what I was missing – a companion, a help-meet… purely altruistically, for the best of reasons, or to drive forward its own plans?

Have I really been curing people? Or have I been bringing it a constant supply of victims? What have I done?

And that's as close as I, the great Doctor Johann Bloom can get to analysis at the moment. For, at the moment, I am simply a man staring in horror at a bundle covered in a blanket and grieving for it. Grieving for my wife. She was real to me. The most wonderful person I ever knew has been taken away from me…

I worked with her for so long. Making this clinic a truly amazing place. Doing what I thought was really wonderful work. Sharing every day with her. Delighting when I made her laugh. Marvelling at how, no matter what the setback, she always knew just what to say. I loved her. I loved her so much. Yet it was all a lie.

And now I know what to do about it.

What Amy Remembered

To be frank, that was easier than I thought it would be. I'd got
Rory back and dispatched a sinister alien duplicate. I was glad
the mist rolled over her quite quickly – I got a glimpse of what
was happening to her, and it wasn't pretty.

I grabbed Rory. The poor lamb was pretty much dead on
his feet. He looked awful. I dragged him up the beach and onto
a sand dune. The storm was all around us – it was really pretty
incredible. Land, sea and sky had joined in one big soggy grey
mush. Fog, rain, whirling sand, you name it, it was all around
us. Wet and choking.

The sea itself was glowing, glowing a bright green that
spread into the mist and the rain.

It looked really bad. And in the middle of it all, madly,
absurdly, were all these dancing figures in ball gowns and wigs
and suits, staggering through the storm like tired clockwork.

I slapped Rory. He opened an eye. 'Amy.' He grinned, and
closed the eye again.

'Lover boy!' I snapped. 'Come on. We've got to stop the
people on the beach from dancing.'

'Really?' he muttered. 'But why… I'm so tired…'

'Because what's happened to you is happening to them.

They're being drained. They're making the storm.'

'Right…' Rory frowned. He stood up and wobbled about a bit. He focused on the beach. 'Blimey.' Then he looked at me. 'Amy, you look great.'

'Thanks, husband.' I nudged him. 'Now come on.'

'Just a second,' he held up a hand. 'Tell me again what you think of my dancing?'

'You are a terrible dancer,' I told him.

Rory nodded. 'Just checking,' he said, a little sadly, bless him. 'Not an alien, then. Let's go stop this.'

It took a while. We dragged people slowly away from their dancers, putting them down in deckchairs. Some of them looked in pretty rough shape. And some of them weren't happy to go.

A little old lady was dancing with a baby. She wouldn't let go of it. She kept crying over and over again.

'Oh, my dears, look at little baby dance! Look at how happy he is! Mummy's ever so tired but she's going to keep on dancing because it makes my little boy laugh. Yes she is, yes she is!'

But we did it, eventually.

Old Mr Nevil, sitting on a deckchair, opened an eye. 'Where did Stoker go?' he muttered. 'That was a lovely dog, you know. Ever so kind natured. Really listened. Where's Olivia gone? Have you seen her?' He slipped off into a deep sleep and started snoring.

Rory's voice called me down to the sea. The baby was grabbing at him. It was floating in mid air, its tiny hands like claws, scratching at his eyes. I ran to him, trying to swat away the child.

'Help!' he cried.

I waded in, and it all went horribly wrong. The baby's tiny

little pudgy hands started digging into my cheeks, its face hissing at me as it pulled at my skin. All the while its mother was yelling at me, hitting me, crying, 'It's my baby! Don't hurt my baby!'

The mist rose up around us and for an instant there was just the strange awful baby, with its little wavy hair and shining eyes and grabby hands. One of them clamped over my nose and mouth, pushing down, stifling me.

'You're not real! You're not real!' I tried to shout, but the creature just shook its head. I felt the blood pounding in my brain and stars began to dance in front of my eyes. I was being suffocated by a flying baby. I stumbled back, my feet splashing in the waves. The baby leered at me, and pressed down harder. I threw my hands up and fell backwards.

In the distance, over the pounding in my ears, I could hear Rory shouting. 'Amy! Amy!' he cried. 'Keep away from the waves...'

The sea was shockingly cold and a livid green, like the brightest pea soup you could ever imagine. And from it hands started to emerge, tugging and pulling at me. I couldn't fight any more, I just couldn't. I needed to breathe, I needed to stand up. I needed...

The baby shifted its entire weight onto my face, forcing my head under the water. My lungs, desperate for air, sucked in great gulps of freezing saltwater and I started to choke. And choked again, and flailed a bit and went under a second time, those weird hands forcing me down.

A hand grabbed me, pulling me up. Rory.

'Am I glad to see you...' I said.

A cry from the shore alerted me. Standing there was Rory. Also.

Right.

Fake Rory.

That was quick.

'Are you all right?' asked the Rory holding my hand. OK. Ten points.

I turned to the Rory on shore. 'What about you, anything to say for yourself?'

'I'm real!' followed by 'Blimey!'

'Yeah, yeah, anything else?'

'Well, at least it's not created a duplicate of the Doctor.'

Hmm. Jealous. Twenty points. And also, a really good point. Sometimes you need a giant alien water brain to tell you what your priorities are.

I turned to the Rory holding my hand. 'So, what have you got to say for yourself, Rory?'

Value Rory looked confused. 'I don't mind about the Doctor, not at all,' he said simply.

'That does it,' I sighed, shoved away the fake, and strode out of the water towards my husband. 'Right then.'

We stood on the sand, surrounded by that glowing mist tugging at our heads.

'What a complete mess,' I said.

Rory nodded.

'How are we doing?'

'We've rescued three dancers.'

'Out of...?'

'Um, a dozen or so. I didn't really count.'

'Grand.' I stared at the empty deckchairs flapping in the wind. 'Storm's still pretty strong, though.'

'Yes.'

'We have to see this as good news. Somehow. The Doctor will get here soon. The Doctor will get here soon.'

'Did somebody call?' That was the Doctor's voice, coming

to us out of the storm.

We ran towards him, calling his name over and over.

There he was. 'Doctor!' I cried out. 'You're OK.'

'Ah,' he said. 'That's a bit of a yes and no.'

The mist cleared around him slightly.

He was held in place by the Elquitine sisters.

'Um,' said the Doctor. 'Meet my guards. For little old dears they're doing rather well.'

The mist cleared some more. Standing a way behind was Prince Boris. Laughing.

'What's happening?' I demanded.

'Ah, Amy,' sighed the Doctor. 'Some days are good days. This is a bad day. Frankly, it's all gone a bit Pete Tong.'

The two ladies dragged the Doctor forward.

'I really wouldn't try and fight them off,' the Doctor warned. 'They're under direct psychic control, I'm afraid. If I get out of this alive I'm going to be bruised till Shrove Tuesday. These two ladies have got a vice-like grip. Well done, girls. I bet you have no problem opening jars.'

They pulled him closer to the water's edge.

'What's happening?' Rory asked.

'Oh,' sighed the Doctor. 'They're going to try and feed me to The Sea. Bad idea, very bad idea.'

They dragged him closer.

A Letter from Maria

St Christophe
7th December 1783

Dear Mother,

I ran down to the beach. It was so cold and so quiet. Everyone stood there, like they were waiting for a game to start – all those grown-ups, all staring at each other.

There were the dancers, all of them frozen still in a circle around the Doctor, who was barely standing, held in place by the Elquitine sisters.

Standing over the crowd was Prince Boris, smiling, waiting, daring someone to say something. He looked so happy, which worried me. I did not care for him any more.

No one seemed to notice me. Apart from Amy, who was mouthing 'Get back, kid.' But I stood where I was. I wanted to watch.

Amy was holding up Rory, who looked pretty bad. Poor monsieur, he looked so tired.

The sea washed in and out around them, glowing and whispering. I could start to hear words in the ocean, muttering and hissing, 'Feed us, give us,' over and over.

It made me shudder, and I worried, Mother – I worried

about all those times you came down here. What happened to you?

What happened NEXT was interesting. In the short time I've known the Doctor, I've seen him do many things. But I've never seen him plead.

He sank to his knees in front of Prince Boris. 'Please,' he begged. 'You mustn't let The Sea scan me. You can't…'

Prince Boris smiled. 'The Sea wants to know very much what's in your head, Doctor. I must admit I'm curious… Already it is reaching out to you…'

The Doctor winced, sharply, like he had a terrible toothache.

Prince Boris's smile grew wide with surprise. 'Why… you have travelled so far… met such amazing people… and a box… such a magical box!' He clapped his hands together. 'These are just the things it can sense by tugging at the very frayed edges of your mind.' He leaned closer to the Doctor, his beard almost scratching the Doctor's nose. 'It wants to know more. It wants to know what's in the depths of your brain. I would let it devour you.'

Quietly, in a whisper that somehow carried across the beach, the Doctor said one word. 'Don't.'

Prince Boris laughed. 'You're a brilliantly funny man. You have a great sense of humour! I like that. I like that very much.'

Suddenly, seemingly without making an effort beyond a shrug, the Doctor was free, standing up. The Elquitine sisters stood back, baffled. Although Prince Boris was a little taller than the Doctor, somehow he stood eye-to-eye with him.

'Don't,' repeated the Doctor, his voice loud and firm. It wasn't a shout but it echoed off the rocks in a way that made me feel so happy. The Doctor was here. Everything would be all right. I noticed Amy and Rory hold hands. It was going to be fine.

The mists parted, drawing back from him, revealing the beach, the patients, Prince Boris looking troubled, and…

Oh, Mother, Dr Bloom was running across the beach. He stopped and stood there, panting heavily. He was crying, crying ever so much. To my amazement, I realised he was holding a GUN.

'You!' he shouted, his hand shaking so much the gun rattled. 'You killed my wife!'

He pulled the trigger, the sound of the shot filling the beach.

The Doctor fell down, an 'Oh' of surprise perfectly matched by the bullet hole in his forehead.

THE DOCTOR'S LAST THOUGHTS

Q: What was the last thing to go through the Doctor's head?

A: A Bullet.

209

WHAT AMY REMEMBERED

I saw the Doctor die.

It was one of those dreadful moments. I once saw a dog crossing the road, not looking where it was going, not seeing a speeding white van. I can remember everything about that – the sign on the van, the happy look on the dog's face, the way it trotted over the road, tongue lolling out between two rows of sharp teeth and red gums, the people on the other side of the street, a special offer in the corner shop, a pram with three shopping bags looped round the handles, a man tying his shoelaces, half a headline from the folded paper on the van's dashboard…

You get the picture. Anyway. The Doctor was dead. As simple as that.

I saw it happen, and it was like my childhood died too. All those hopes and adventures and ideas, all dropped to the ground with him. It was the Doctor and someone had just shot him. Not a clone, a duplicate, a copy or an imitation. Not a glancing blow, not a flesh wound, not a blank or a near-miss but an unquestionably deadly shot. Dr Bloom had just had the most amazing bit of beginner's luck. Funny how you think stuff like that.

My first impulse was to ask the Doctor what he thought of it all, as he'd be bound to have something funny to say. Something really funny and Doctory. Funny and Doctory and really reassuring. Instead, he said nothing. He just lay in a little dead heap on the wet sand. Because he was dead. My raggedy Doctor.

My second impulse was to turn to Rory, whose hand I was gripping ever so tightly.

'Do something!' I yelled.

The Story of Rory

The Doctor was dead.

Amy started shouting. I don't think she even realised she was doing it. You know when they show on the news those women who have just lost their entire families under a mudslide? It was that kind of noise. Just grief without words because there were just no words that suited.

It wasn't even the kind of noise that did anything. I'd like to say the noise shattered glass or something. But it didn't. It was just loud and horrible.

She gripped my hand, really, really tightly, crushing it. I let her. It was all I could do. I just stared at the Doctor lying on the shore, the waves edging towards him. He'd been so tall a second ago. Now he was tiny, like he wasn't real. Rain was already soaking his clothes.

Over Amy's screaming, I could hear a strange little clickety-clickety noise, over and over. It was Dr Bloom's hand shaking so much the gun rattled. His face... he looked as though he didn't know what he'd done. He was just shocked. He looked so unhappy, I wanted to run to him. Only I couldn't. Because I was holding Amy, and I would never let her go.

Funny that. The most amazing person in the universe

drops dead in front of you and I wanted to go and hug the man who'd done it because he looked so sad.

The gun fell out of his hands and onto the beach with a wet slap. Dr Bloom looked up at Prince Boris. 'There,' he cried. 'Are you happy now?'

Prince Boris waggled a hand equivocally. 'So-So,' he rumbled. 'The Sea very much wanted the Doctor's brain. I just found him rather annoying.'

'He killed my wife,' murmured Bloom, his voice simple. 'You told me he would. I wasn't able to prevent it. I had to do something.'

'I know,' Prince Boris sounded bored. 'You were supposed to shoot him earlier. It's a bit late now.'

'Yes,' said Dr Bloom miserably. 'Yes.'

The Doctor just lay there on the beach. The initial shock was fading, and I was starting to realise a few troubling things. Funny how selfish you really are. If the Doctor was dead, that meant we were stranded here. Living out the rest of our lives in the past. With no decent plumbing and terrible food and… oh yeah, the French Revolution just about to start. What would we do? How would we make a living? What if the TARDIS turned up – could we get back into it? Would Amy be able to fly it? How would we get back to Leadworth? Was that even where Amy would want to go?

Her pressure on my hand grew. 'Do something,' she cried.

Which was, in the circumstances, the least helpful thing she could have said. I mean, what? But my medical training kicked in. I went to his body, rolling it over. It was amazing how neat that little bullet hole was, how pale the Doctor's face was. Strange – I've never seen his face at rest before. Even when he's thinking hard, or staring at you, his face is moving, alive. But this wasn't. It was dead.

I felt his heart. And then his other one. The other, annoying, impossibly wrong one. Nothing. There was no point to any of this. Gunshot to the head.

I even found myself giving him artificial respiration. Funny that – kissing the Doctor. Really, you know, should have been Amy. Kissing him goodbye. But maybe, just maybe – I mean, he was an alien. Maybe he didn't keep his brain in his head. Maybe that was where he kept an appendix or something else a bit useless. Maybe he was fine. Just needed a bit of TLC, bringing back to life.

Nothing. Absolutely nothing.

I felt Amy's hand on me. Gentler this time. Just resting on my shoulder. She was crying.

'Rory,' she sniffed. 'It's OK. You can stop.'

But I didn't. Not for a bit.

Eventually, I stood up, letting Amy wrap her arms around me. We looked at the Doctor's body.

'Bet this isn't what he had in mind,' I said.

Amy sniffed, almost laughing.

Prince Boris was still standing there, gently amused by the whole thing. Wasn't it Russians who made bears fight each other? Have I got that one wrong?

That look on his face – bored triumph. That was what did it.

I decided – This wasn't the end.

I'd had the Doctor in my head. I knew what heroes did. It was time to be one.

WHAT AMY REMEMBERED

I love Rory Williams.

He stood up to The Sea. He picked up the Doctor by the shoulders and he turned to The Sea and he shouted, 'Heal him! Go on! Heal him!'

Rory started hauling the Doctor into the surf, the waves dragging around him. I ran to him and we both held the Doctor up while The Sea surged around us, the water green and greedy. Lights boiled under the surface.

We kept the Doctor there, limp in our arms, feeling the fog press in, The Sea tug and drag at him.

'Heal him!' Rory yelled again, and this time I joined in.

'Go on! He's what you've been after all this time! Do it!' I waited a second and then added, a bit lamely, 'Please.'

I hoped it was going to be all right. I really hoped it was going to be all right.

Remember that dog that got run over? I can still see the van driver cradling it and saying the same thing over and over, really desperately hoping that it was all going to be OK.

Now here's Amy Pond, standing in the freezing ocean, holding the dead body of her imaginary friend, and shouting at the sea to make him better.

Yeah. If only my therapists could see me now.

That was it for a bit. I could sense that Prince Boris and Dr Bloom were watching us. Prince Boris was probably amused – you know, in that 'English people are sooo funny' way of his. Dr Bloom looked like the lights were off and no one was home any more.

Then The Sea… it surged up around the Doctor. Rory and I fell back, or were pushed back – I'm not really sure. But we fell against the shore, winded and soaked.

Rory helped me up and we both stood there, shaking with shock and cold. There was no sign of the Doctor. Just thick fog everywhere.

Then the fog cleared slightly, and showed us that The Sea looked wrong, somehow. It was a livid green – the shade of green you dye your hair when you're 14 years old and a bit rebellious. It lit up the sky the same sickly colour. And it was boiling and thrashing like a kettle full of angry squid.

Then The Sea parted, splitting down the middle and rushing away, leaving the Doctor's huddled body lying on a pile of rocks, surrounded by a thick wall of churning water that hissed and spat.

Amazingly, the little figure stood up.

The Doctor was alive.

I held on to Rory, ever so tightly. My hero.

The Doctor ignored the giant, impossible water feature in front of him and turned around. He waved absently at Prince Boris and Dr Bloom – it was the kind of wave that said 'I'll deal with you in a minute'. Instead he faced Rory and me.

'Hello!' he said.

'Hello,' we said back. Bit lame. Couldn't think of anything else to say.

'Rory Williams.' The Doctor stuck his hands in his pockets,

pulled out a fish, frowned at it, and threw it away. 'Rory, Rory, Rory – was it your idea to get The Sea to cure me?'

'Yes,' said Rory, smiling.

'That was brilliant.' The Doctor beamed, then his face fell. '-ly awful.'

'What?'

'The one thing I have been trying very hard not to do was to let The Sea scan me.'

'I didn't have any choice!' protested Rory. 'You were dead! I wasn't giving up on you! I wasn't letting them win!'

'Never mind,' sighed the Doctor. Truthfully, I thought he was being a tad ungrateful. 'Now… Just run.'

One of the things you learn very quickly around the Doctor is never to question him when he says that word. You just run. It's almost like breathing.

As we started running, something really, really terrible happened to The Sea.

The Doctor was just standing there. He was screaming at the top of his voice. He was arguing with The Sea. 'I am sorry!' he was yelling. 'I've been trying very hard to stop this happening.'

The Sea made a noise.

It was as if water could scream.

The Doctor's voice got even louder. 'Your Familiars work by reading people's minds and becoming what they miss the most. You do all that and you take on all their pain, everything they've done, and you give them back something they've lost. Which is why I knew I could never let you anywhere near me. I've tried so hard.'

The Sea screamed again, bulging and tearing itself around him.

'I've lived so long. I've lost so much.' The Doctor reached

out a hand, beseeching the shuddering waves. 'I'm the very worst thing you could possibly have scanned.'

A wind howled, knocking us all flat, blasting sand into our eyes. I tried to keep watching – through the storm I could just see The Sea twisting and turning, reaching out and forming itself into something... almost unnameably horrible. A giant towering creature – tentacles, and claws and teeth and metal and hundreds of mouths. All screaming. The creature still changing and shifting and howling reared up, blocking out the sky, tearing the wind from the air. It was bubbling and thrashing and expanding and dissolving – in places there were what looked like struggling limbs and howling faces, in others it appeared to be sprouting shiny silver towers, and shapes I just couldn't describe – just a giant nightmarish confusion that was growing bigger and bigger and more and more agonised.

Over its cries, I could hear the Doctor shouting at the top of his lungs: 'I'm the Last of the Time Lords.' His voice dropped grimly. 'Unexpected Item in the Bagging Area.'

Then the beach exploded.

A LETTER FROM MARIA

St Christophe
8th December 1783

Dear Mother,

I woke up from a long sleep. The Doctor was building a sandcastle. He saw me looking at him and he smiled.

'Hello Maria,' he said. 'Everyone else is still asleep. It's been a long night.'

I stood up and realised my dress was covered in sand. I brushed it off me and looked about. The beach was covered with sleeping bodies. Amy and Rory were holding each other, the patients lay dotted about in clumps. It was a beautiful clear morning. The first I can remember in ever so long. The sea stretched out for miles to a clear blue horizon. Gulls bobbed lazily on the surface of the water.

I went over to help the Doctor with his sandcastle, but he held up a stern finger. 'Now then, Maria, these things have to be done properly…' he explained. I looked. It was a marvellous castle with battlements and turrets and windows.

Sadly I said, 'Monsieur, it is finished, is it not?'

He shook his head. 'What good is a castle without people?'

So we built some people out of sand.

He made a princess which looked a little bit like me. I tried making some soldiers, but they were very lumpy. I got better. 'What about the other people on the beach?'

The Doctor looked up and down the beach. 'They're sleeping off a vast psychic trauma, so best not to be moved. But they'll be fine. I've checked. I popped back inside and borrowed the odd blanket. After all they've been through, it seemed a shame to let them catch cold.' He sighed and patted down a brave knight on a horse.

We carried on making sand people. 'There. All lovely and perfect.' He paused. 'What are those, Maria?'

I pointed to my forces. 'This is the invading army that's attacking the castle. You've got to have them.'

The Doctor sighed. 'Yes, I guess you must.'

He looked so sad that I said, 'Monsieur, I can just get rid of them if you want. They're only sand.'

He shook his head, and seemed so old and tired. 'No Maria, you're right.'

We sat in silence for a bit.

'What about Amy and Rory?' I asked.

The Doctor smiled. 'They're too old for sandcastles.'

'What's the point of this castle?' I asked. 'Won't the sea wash it away?'

The Doctor frowned. 'Just the kind of thing Amy would say,' he sighed. 'Maybe you're getting too old for sandcastles too.' He tapped me on the nose and smiled sadly.

I shook my head. He was a funny man.

He started to dig a moat. 'You make a good enough moat, it holds the sea off for a little while longer. It's not great, but it's the best I can manage.' He leaned back on his heels. 'Sometimes that's the most you can hope for.'

'What happened to everyone?' I asked him.

'Oh,' he looked as though he wished I hadn't asked him. 'Ah. Well. The sea was host to a rare and beautiful creature. It was trying its best. But it wasn't well. It was wounded. It was reaching out, trying to find a mind to control it – that's what it's used to. First it found Dr Bloom, but he wasn't strong enough. And then it found Prince Boris. It made him... well, it made him everything he'd never got around to being. It cured his illness, but also his laziness. Which sounds silly. But really all that was stopping him from being very unpleasant was thinking there wasn't much point in bothering. You people are strange and silly.'

(Yes, Mother, he really did say 'you people', which was ever such an odd thing to say when you think about it.)

'As soon as I arrived, I could sense that creature poking around in my head – and I knew what it was and that it mustn't be allowed to read my mind. It really mustn't. The things I've lost, the things I've seen... trying to make those tore it apart. It was such a lovely, noble, gentle creature, really. I tried to save it.' He let out a long breath, almost a wail. 'I didn't do very well.' He peered out to the sea, to the tiniest, faintest green shimmer on the surface. 'There's only perhaps the ghost of it left.'

I patted him on the arm. 'You tried, monsieur.'

He took my hand and squeezed it. 'Thank you.'

With a loud skitter of sand, Amy came running up, spraying sand into the moat as she thudded to a halt.

'Oi!' she cried out to the Doctor. 'Making sandcastles? What are you, five?'

Extract from a Letter from Prince Boris

… and so ended, my dear Andrei, your brother's plan to take over the world!

Up until today, I thought it was only you and dear Mother who knew me for what I really was (although she always took my side, bless her). But then, I realised the Doctor knew me.

I woke up in bed, and he was sitting there, reading a paper. I nodded to him.

'Hello!' he said. 'No, no, don't try and get up – I'm afraid you were closest to the psychic blast. Probably sent your spinal column jangling like a wind chime.'

I was rueful. 'I imagine this means I won't avoid the lecture.'

To my surprise he shrugged. 'Do you really want one? You know, I've spent hundreds of years arguing with people like you. Do you know, in all that time, not one of you lot has ever changed your mind? It's like arguing with the internet.' He grinned. 'Don't worry, I'm not wasting either of our breaths.'

I laughed with him until his smile faded.

'So,' he said, 'in case you were wondering, let me see – the poor creature you were trying to exploit is gone. As is your mental link to the patients. Nothing left. It's a terrible, terrible waste. Happy?'

'Not really, but it was worth a try,' I said, straightening out the bedspread.

'Really?' he leapt to his feet. 'Honestly? That's it.'

'These things are always worth a try.' I waggled a hand. 'You never know.'

'Nah,' he said. 'Trouble is, I always do know. I always win. And no, it doesn't get boring.'

'This is starting to sound perilously like a lecture, my dear Doctor,' I put in, yawning.

He nodded. 'I just wanted to know… have you always been like this? Always? Really?'

I spread out my hands. 'For my sins.'

'Now you're just being charming,' The Doctor started pacing angrily. 'I mean, what did you really imagine would happen? That you'd rule the world? Because I tell you this, from here on in there's a lot of that going around. It suddenly gets fashionable. Few years from now a Frenchman will try it. I kid you not.'

We both laughed at this.

I tugged at the counterpane again. 'I'll tell you the truth, Doctor. I've always been this way… but there just didn't seem that much point. You know, what's the point when you're going to drop dead any day? And then, all of a sudden, when I started to feel better, when I realised how powerful the creature was, and what I could do with it…'

'I know,' the Doctor agreed with me. He told me how, if he had the power, he'd use it to destroy whole worlds and not give it a second thought. Well, that's not quite what he said, but those were pretty much his sentiments.

'I admire you,' said the Doctor. 'No, no, I really do. To be given a second chance, and to so utterly, totally, awfully miss the point.'

'That's where you're wrong,' I argued. 'You missed the point. I took the risk. It's what makes me the great man, and you the tiny one.'

The Doctor shrugged. 'Well, I like being tiny.'

He stared at me then. His eyes not even blinking. Almost as though they didn't need to.

'Well,' he said. 'As you said, you took a risk.'

'And look how I lost,' I sighed. 'With a bit of luck, I could have lived for ever.'

'Instead of which…' The Doctor pulled a face.

'It's all right,' I said. 'I know. The cure is fading.'

'What will you do now?' he asked.

'Oh, make the most of the time I have left. Hopefully finish reading a few books.'

'Better make them short ones.' He nodded. 'Well, I have to go and sort out the mess. But I thought I'd make sure that you were all right.'

'Generous in victory?' I asked.

'Not exactly,' he said. 'It's just such a shame. As I said, I really liked you.'

We both laughed again at that. Then my laugh turned into a cough. The coughing lasted a very long time.

When I finished coughing and looked up, the Doctor had gone…

What Amy Remembered

This is the story of how it ended. The sun, such as it was, made its appearance through the glass roof of the porch. It was a cold wintry light. A grimly silent gathering of patients sat around while the Elquitine sisters played a mournful requiem.

The Doctor came in, trying to ignore the accusing glances from everyone. He joined Rory and me at a table away from the fire. He didn't say anything.

'So,' Rory asked eventually, 'everything's all tidied away, then, is it?'

The Doctor grimaced. 'History is back on track. Messy and not enough of a happy ending for anyone, really.'

I jerked a hand at the patients. I tried not to meet Olivia Elquitine's accusing glare. 'How will they be?'

'Well, actually… as good as possible,' said the Doctor. He was putting a brave face on it. 'Some will stay cured… and some will not. Depends on what it was trying to mend, what it had to work with. I'll be fine, so will Rory. And those who've left the clinic… but those still being cured?' He sighed. 'Well, they'll have to trust Dr Bloom. Fresh air, hygiene, countryside… it's all very forward thinking. It's probably adding years to their lives – and it's all Dr Bloom's work. So

I'm not going to interfere – this is history playing out as it should do.'

'Really?'

'Really,' said the Doctor, not meeting our eyes. 'Well,' he muttered, 'kind of.' He realised we were staring at him. 'What am I supposed to do, go around bumping them all off?'

'Good luck,' said Rory. 'The Elquitine sisters would take you down.'

The Doctor nodded at that. 'Try and think of it not so much a happy ending as a less sad one.'

I looked at his face, so pulled down and tired. 'Prince Boris?' I asked.

The Doctor puffed out some air and looked down to the sea. 'A very charming man. I should be more careful of very charming men.' He tugged a smile from his lips. 'At least I don't have that problem with you, Rory.'

'Oi,' said Rory.

'What are we doing about the TARDIS?'

'Oh, it'll turn up. Like a late train it's probably just around the corner.'

'You hope.' I grinned at him.

'Well, otherwise we could get jobs here.'

We stared at him.

'Just not in France. Not for a while. No.'

He leaned back in his chair. For once it didn't topple over. 'Result,' he said.

A Letter from Maria

St Christophe
9th December 1783

Dear Mother,

So the Doctor made all the monsters go away. Can I come home now? I miss you so much. I have decided that we should call the puppies Rory and Amy.

Your ever loving

Maria

A LETTER FROM MR NEVIL

Dear Octavius,

Well, there's good news and there's bad news, you dear old fraud.

The bad news is that the cure is fading. The good news is that I'm not coming home. So you won't have to face my wrath and the horse-whipping you soundly deserve.

No, I shall see my days out here at St Christophe – the air is good and I have made friends. I think, you know, I have found peace and companionship here – although perhaps I shall not go for many walks along the beach.

It's a good winter – the climate is chilly but not too cold, although it looks as though there may be snow falling on the sea. The foreign girl is talking to me again and the sawbones who runs this place is a good enough soul, I suppose. Deserves a chance. Who knows, I may see out the spring…

Your faithful servant,

Henry Nevil

DR BLOOM'S JOURNAL

There was a knock at the door. The Doctor brought in a tea tray.

'Good morning, Dr Bloom,' he said.

I didn't answer, just stared out at the shore.

Eventually he spoke again. 'I am sorry about your wife.'

'And I am sorry I shot you.'

'Well, there we are.' The Doctor settled the tray down with a bang. 'All friends, then. Let's call it quits.'

This was the man who'd killed my wife. And he was sitting opposite me, smiling. I had killed him. I had made the decision. I'd pulled the trigger. I had decided to live with the consequences, and yet here he was.

The Doctor handed me something. It wasn't tea.

'You're in shock,' he said gently. 'I think it's brandy or sherry. Try it. It's nice. Well, it's brown.'

I tried to sip from the glass, but my hands were shaking. I put the glass down.

The Doctor was crouching in front of my chair, staring into my face. He wasn't blinking at all. 'I am so sorry. Look, I could say, "Prince Boris made me do it." He manipulated us all. A brilliant strategist. But I thought I was doing the right thing. In a way…'

'She was my wife.'

The Doctor shook his head, and repeated his lies. That she wasn't. That she'd been in my life for a matter of months, an invention, a fiction. Something to control me, to make me trust the creature on the beach. All lies. I had known Perdita for… I had known Perdita… Perdita, the only woman who had ever trusted, believed or liked me.

And she wasn't real.

'Take your time,' said the Doctor.

I realised the sun was setting. It does that ever so quickly in winter.

'I know what you must think of me,' he said, his voice so slow. It was like a voice designed for laughing that didn't get to do it often. 'I'm going to tell you a story about a man who travels, and everywhere he goes, he makes everyone's lives better. I'm not that man. That man doesn't exist. I wish he did.' He smiled. 'I'd believe in him.'

He tapped me on the knee.

'I just try my best. I really do. Just like you – you are brilliant, you're doing wonderful things. It's people like you who will wipe out a terrible, terrible disease – but you're not the man to do it. Doesn't mean you shouldn't try. It will take time. A hundred years from now, places like this will be everywhere, and people will really understand the disease – but it takes a man like you to make that happen, to really sit down and have a think rather than telling people that they're vampires, or should drink tar or…' He stopped.

'I was so close,' I said. I noticed there wasn't any expression in my voice. Just hope.

'I know,' he said. 'But you weren't, really. You'd just gone racing down a really fun-looking blind alley. Happens to us all. You thought you were curing a plague, but you were accidentally unleashing something much worse on the world… and for the best, the very best of reasons.' He sighed. 'I hate days like this.'

'Could she have lived?'

The Doctor shook his head. 'You were powering her. She was powering you.'

'And my patients?'

He stood and stared out of the window. 'Weather's not too bad for winter, really, is it? Quite mild, all things considered.'

I knew then that was the best answer I'd get from this strange man.

He started absently fiddling with my desk, tidying it. He stopped suddenly, holding up a sheet of paper.

'What's this?' he asked.

'What it looks like,' I said.

He picked up sheet after sheet of paper, all from a neatly folded pile.

A pile of letters.

'Maria?' he smiled, flicking through them. 'She's been writing all this down? Oh, bless her. She's got a lovely turn of phrase for an 11-year-old.' He leafed on through the pile. 'Although that's not how that happened… and no, she's wrong, bow ties are cool.' He paused, and tutted at me. 'You shouldn't read other people's letters, though,' he admonished, before carrying on reading.

'I haven't been,' I groaned. 'I don't read them any more.'

'Then why have you been keeping her letters?' He was cross. 'Surely you post these on to her mother?'

I shook my head. 'No, I am afraid we do not.'

The Doctor stopped, his hand shaking in mid air. 'Why not?'

I chose my words carefully, like picking my way along an icy path. 'The child's mother does not wish any further contact with her.'

'She's abandoned her?' The Doctor was outraged. 'Just because she's ill, her own mother's disowned her? That's inhuman. She's a patient, not an orphan.'

'She's not the patient, Doctor.' I paused. 'Her mother was.'

The Doctor stopped. He picked up a letter and scanned through it, reading the words over and over. '*I am feeling better now... why am I here... when will I see you again?*'

I remembered that last day, the mother, packed and crying, waiting for the carriage, and Maria skipping about, all excited about going back to Paris.

Her mother looked at me, agonised. I stepped forward. 'Maria, my dear, I am just the tiniest bit worried about your temperature.' I laid a hand on the child's forehead. 'Yes. It's a little high. I'm so sorry, but I cannot, I just cannot allow you to travel with your mother. For your own good. Not just yet.'

'But Mother!' protested Maria, not seeing the look on her mother's face.

Maria started to cry. My dear Perdita hurried forward. 'Now, now, Maria,' she said. 'We're all worried about you – the filthy air of Paris... It's no good, you know. It just won't do. I really must insist. Just for a little while, until you are Quite Right.' Maria looked up at her and, I genuinely think, started to hate her there and then.

'Madame Bloom is right,' Maria's mother said to me, her eyes shining with tears. 'Perhaps you might stay on.' She paused, her face showing that she was in two minds. 'I suppose... I suppose she must, mustn't she, Dr Bloom?' She faltered, indecision clear on her face.

My Perdita simply nodded, gripping hold of the girl by the

shoulders as Maria's mother climbed into that carriage and drove away.

Maria's last words to her were, 'I may write to you, Mother, mayn't I?'

All this I remembered with sadness.

'Her mother was one of my earliest patients, Doctor. When she got well… she left Maria behind. It was almost like she got well so as to get away from her, from the pain of seeing her again. It was too much for her.'

The Doctor's voice was hollow and so sad. 'Maria has no idea, does she?'

'The poor woman fell ill soon after losing her daughter. The Sea was able to read her ever so well. It gave her back her daughter. Who healed her.'

The Doctor sat down on a chair, staring at me. Holding that last letter.

'I'm sorry, Doctor. Maria is just a creature of The Sea. She's not real.'

A Letter from Maria

St Christophe
10th December 1783

Dear Mother,

It's quiet around here, except for the coughing. I'm so lonely – now that the Doctor and Amy and Rory are going away. Can I come home now? I miss you so much. I don't want to be here alone.

Your ever loving

Maria

Epilogue
The Story of Rory

You know what? The Doctor doesn't always get it right, and he doesn't save everyone. Sometimes it's like Amy's blind to that. She can see him, shining like the angel on a Christmas tree – she just doesn't see how hard his eyes sometimes are, and how he sometimes keeps on laughing when the joke's stopped being funny.

That last morning, Amy came running up from the beach to say that the TARDIS had reappeared from wherever it went to. The Doctor rushed down there immediately, obviously. He tried to act like he was all nonchalant and didn't care, but really he was off like a shot. I suppose it's his home and his oldest friend. When Amy and I are long gone, he'll still have his magic blue Narnia cupboard.

I stayed, for one last breakfast. I'd like to say it was for the food, but really it was to say goodbye to all the people the Doctor's forgotten about. The Elquitine sisters came to my table. Olivia was wheezing away. Her sister was so weary and looked like a bony broom.

Mr Nevil hovered nearby. I'd noticed he couldn't leave Olivia alone. Kind of sweet – the old tartar was mellowing. He looked like he wanted to intercede, but Olivia warded him off with a stern glance. What she had to say was family business.

They sat at my table with difficulty. 'Young man, I hear you're leaving us?'

I nodded.

'Well, then,' she said, folding her hands tightly. 'My sister has something to say. Something for the Doctor. Can you pass it on?'

I nodded again. I realised I'd never heard Helena speak.

'She's been saving her breath up for him,' said Olivia, proudly. 'But I suspect he's not coming back, is he?'

I realised the truth of it as soon as she said it. 'No,' I replied. She nodded tightly.

The thin sister reached forward, grabbing my hand in her bony claw. 'Tell him… Tell him… I hate him,' she said, and leaned back, panting and exhausted from the effort.

'Goes for me, too,' said Olivia, reaching for a pastry.

I headed down to the beach, where Maria and Amy were running around on the sand. Amy broke away and grabbed me in a hug. 'That's my Rory boy!' she said, giving me a squeeze.

'It really is freezing down here,' I said.

'And that's my Rory boy complaining,' said Amy, nudging Maria, who laughed.

Maria looked at the TARDIS. Clearly the Doctor was inside. 'Is that really your carriage?' She asked. 'It is not very good, monsieur. It has no wheels.'

'It doesn't need them,' laughed Amy. 'It's an English carriage. They don't have wheels.'

'Does Monsieur Rory push it?'

'When necessary,' laughed Amy.

We fell silent. We were clearly all waiting for the Doctor

to come out of the box. A bit awkward, like waiting for a bus that's just a bit delayed.

Instead the Doctor stuck his head around the back of the TARDIS. He was grinning.

'Maria!' he said. 'I've a surprise for you!'

Maria looked at him, doubtfully. 'An English surprise?'

The Doctor shook his head. 'No, no, no. Why would I give you one of those? It'd be rubbish. This is a fine and lovely Paris surprise.'

The Doctor stepped forward, bringing with him an elegant woman in a cloak.

Maria gasped and ran forward. 'Mother!' she cried, clinging to the woman's skirts.

The woman reached down, and kissed her daughter. 'Oh my dear love,' she said. 'I have missed you. You look wonderfully well.'

'I know! I have ever so many things to tell you! Isn't the Doctor the most amazing man! He's ever so clever – he has such a brain!'

Maria's mother looked at the Doctor, and for a moment her face was cold and blank, as though she didn't like him much. 'Indeed,' was all she said, though.

'Can we go back to Paris?' asked Maria.

Her mother shook her head. 'No, indeed, I rather think we shall travel for a bit. See a few countries.' She bowed stiffly to us. 'Come along,' she said with a smile for her daughter. 'St Christophe's this way – I have a fancy to hire a carriage.'

'Did you not bring one with you?'

Maria's mother smiled tightly. 'No, I'm afraid I have been walking along the sea front with the Doctor. He has been explaining many things to me.'

With that, she took Maria's hand and walked away. And if

her mother's feet didn't quite reach the ground, Maria didn't seem to notice at all.

The Doctor opened the door of the TARDIS. 'As I said, only a ghost of it remained. Just enough for one more Familiar. A marvellous creature. It needed something to do in life.' He ushered us in. 'Someone to love.'

Amy ran to the console. We watched her go. The Doctor turned to me, studying my face.

'How are you, Rory?' he asked.

I looked over at Amy before I answered him. 'It's been odd being you.'

'Isn't it?' The Doctor's smile didn't quite reach his eyes.

'How do you cope?'

'Ah…' The Doctor picked away at a scrap of loose paint on the door. 'Well, I just get as close as I can to a happy ending, then I shut the door behind me and move on.'

I nodded.

We shut the door behind us and moved on.

Also available in the Doctor Who History Collection:

THE STONE ROSE
JACQUELINE RAYNER
ISBN 978 1 849 90906 8

A 2,000 year old statue of Rose Tyler is a mystery that the Doctor and Rose can only solve by travelling back to the time when it was made. But when they do, they find the mystery is deeper and more complicated than they ever imagined.

While the Doctor searches for a missing boy, Rose befriends a girl who it seems can accurately predict the future. But when the Doctor stumbles on the terrible truth behind the statue, Rose herself learns that you have to be very careful what you wish for.

An adventure set in Roman times, featuring the Tenth Doctor, as played by David Tennant, and his companion Rose Tyler.

Also available in the Doctor Who *History Collection:*

THE WITCH HUNTERS
STEVE LYONS
ISBN 978 1 849 90902 0

With the Doctor wanting to repair the TARDIS in peace and
quiet, Barbara, Ian and Susan decide to get some experience
of living in the nearby village of Salem. But the Doctor knows
about the horrors destined to engulf the village and determines
that they should leave.

His friends are not impressed. His granddaughter Susan has
her own ideas, and is desperate to return, whatever the cost.
But perhaps the Doctor was right. Perhaps Susan's actions will
lead them all into terrible danger and cause the tragedy that is
already unfolding to escalate out of control.

An adventure set during the seventeenth-century Salem Witch Trials,
featuring the First Doctor, as played by William Hartnell, and his
companions Susan, Ian and Barbara.

Also available in the Doctor Who *History Collection:*

HUMAN NATURE
PAUL CORNELL
ISBN 978 1 849 90909 9

Hulton College in Norfolk is a school dedicated to producing military officers. With the First World War about to start, the boys of the school will soon be on the front line. But no one expects a war – not even Dr John Smith, the college's new house master…

The Doctor's friend Benny is enjoying her holiday in the same town. But then she meets a future version of the Doctor, and things start to get dangerous very quickly. With the Doctor she knows gone, and only a suffragette and an elderly rake for company, can Benny fight off a vicious alien attack? And will Dr Smith be able to save the day?

An adventure set in Britain on the eve of the First World War, featuring the Seventh Doctor, as played by Sylvester McCoy, and his companion Bernice Summerfield. This book was the basis for the Tenth Doctor television story Human Nature / The Family of Blood *starring David Tennant.*

Also available in the Doctor Who History Collection:

THE ENGLISH WAY OF DEATH
GARETH ROBERTS
ISBN 978 1 849 90908 2

The Doctor, Romana and K-9 are hoping for a holiday in
London in the sweltering summer of 1930. But the TARDIS is
warning of time pollution. And that's not the only problem.

What connects the isolated Sussex resort of Nutchurch with
the secret society run by the eccentric Percy Closed? Why
has millionaire Hepworth Stackhouse dismissed his staff and
hired assassin Julia Orlostro? And what is the truth behind the
infernal vapour known only as Zodaal?

With the heat building, the Doctor and his friends set out to
solve the mysteries.

*An adventure set in 1930s London, featuring the Fourth Doctor, as
played by Tom Baker, and his companions Romana and K-9.*

Also available in the Doctor Who *History Collection:*

THE SHADOW IN THE GLASS
JUSTIN RICHARDS AND STEPHEN COLE

ISBN 978 1 849 90905 1

When a squadron of RAF Hurricanes shoots down an
unidentified aircraft over Turelhampton, the village is
immediately evacuated. But why is the village still guarded by
troops in 2001? When a television documentary crew break
through the cordon looking for a story, they find they've
recorded more than they'd bargained for.

Caught up in both a deadly conspiracy and a historical mystery,
retired Brigadier Lethbridge-Stewart calls upon his old friend
the Doctor. Half-glimpsed demons watch from the shadows as
the Doctor and the Brigadier travel back in time to discover the
last, and deadliest, secret of the Second World War.

*An adventure set partly in the Second Wold War, featuring the Sixth
Doctor, as played by Colin Baker, and Brigadier Lethbridge-Stewart.*

Also available in the Doctor Who *History Collection:*

AMORALITY TALE
DAVID BISHOP
ISBN 978 1 849 90904 4

When gangster Tommy Ramsey is released from prison,
he is determined to retake control of his East End territory.
But new arrivals threaten his grip on illegal activity in the
area. An evangelical minister is persuading people to seek
redemption for their sins. A new gang is claiming the streets.
And a watchmender called Smith is leading a revolt against the
Ramsey Mob's protection racket.

When Tommy strikes back at his enemies, a far more terrifying
threat is revealed. Within hours the city's air turns into nerve
gas and thousands succumb to the choking fumes. London is
dying…

*An adventure set in 1950s London, featuring the Third Doctor, as played
by Jon Pertwee, and his companion Sarah Jane Smith.*